MATCH ME if you CAN

Also by Lindzee Armstrong

NO MATCH FOR LOVE SERIES

Miss Match

Not Your Match

Mix 'N Match

Matched by Design

Match Me if You Can

Match Me by Christmas

Never Say Match

Match Me Again

Mistakenly Matched

My Fake Match

Mistletoe Match

Strike a Match

Meet Your Match

ROYAL SECRETS SERIES

Taming the Prince

Dating the Prince

Winning Back the Princess

Marrying the King

CHRISTMAS IN SNOWBROOK CREEK SERIES

Sleigh Bells and Saddles

MATCH ME if YOU CAN

a No Match for Love romance

USA TODAY BESTSELLING AUTHOR
LINDZEE ARMSTRONG

Chapter One

Never before had a wedding made Tamera so miserable. Her seven a.m. flight out of Texas and back to L.A. couldn't come soon enough.

Her eyes trailed around the crowded ballroom. This entire reception was ripped right from her virtual wedding vision board. The four-foot-tall table centerpieces of white orchids with sprigs of jeweled crystals were almost identical to the ones she had admired online two years ago. The raised dance floor shimmered under the spotlights with painted glitter, just like she'd always imagined it would. The ice cream sundae bar even had chalkboard tags. Katie had stolen all of Tamera's ideas, then made them gross by picking lavender as her primary wedding color.

She'd never believed Katie would take their sibling rivalry this far.

A heavy hand landed on Tamera's upper back, and she looked up at her date. Drew's dirty-blond hair hung halfway down his broad back in a loose ponytail, and his massive hand held out a glass of champagne.

"Thanks," Tamera said, accepting the beverage.

"No problem."

Drew sank into the chair beside hers, looking out of place in a suit and tie instead of his usual football jersey and jeans. He hadn't wanted to come to the wedding, but Tamera's begging finally convinced him.

After spending nearly twelve weeks in each other's constant presence, she'd learned Drew's weak points and how to exploit them.

"How much longer until we can get out of here?" Drew asked.

Tamera took a long sip of the chilled alcohol, trying to cool the fury that had her seeing red at every stolen detail. The lavender silk of her maid of honor dress burned like hot oil. This was the trashier, tackier version of the day she'd always imagined having herself. Right down to the groom.

At least photos of her and Drew at the wedding would look great on social media. Her followers would eat it up.

"You promised you'd stay until the bitter end. You're my arm candy tonight so I don't look pathetic." Tamera knew without a doubt that photos of tonight would go viral on social media, whether she wanted them to or not.

Drew wiggled his eyebrows up and down. "Say the word, and we can make that agreement a little more permanent."

Tamera rolled her eyes and tossed back the rest of her champagne. She and Drew had met over the summer on *Eye in the Sky*, a reality TV show where twenty contestants competed for a million dollars while locked in a glass house covered with cameras. The network had contrived a showmance between her and Drew, but it'd never been more than harmless flirtations on his part and reluctant flattery on hers. The sting of Caleb's betrayal was still too fresh for Tamera to even consider a relationship. Still, she and Drew had allied themselves in the game and become close friends by the time they were both voted out near the end of the season.

"Friends only," Tamera reminded Drew. She was pretty sure he was only interested in her because she'd said no, anyway. The quarterback of the San Antonio Vigilantes could have any girl he wanted, even if an injury would keep him benched for most of the upcoming season.

His arm landed heavily around her shoulders. "How about friends with benefits?"

She laughed and pushed his arm off. "In your dreams."

"You sure know how to make a guy feel special."

The words sliced through her, and she looked away so he wouldn't see how they hurt. She had tried her hardest to be a good girlfriend to

2

Caleb. Sure, they'd had their share of problems, but she'd really thought they were happy. How could he have carried on an affair—with her sister, no less—for an entire year without her knowing? She might as well have walked around with #oblivious stamped on her forehead. Followers had said as much in their numerous comments on her page.

The DJ announced that the bride and groom would now share their first dance. Tension spread down Tamera's neck and over her shoulders. An overly romantic pop song crackled over the speakers, then pulsed through the room at a near deafening decibel.

No freaking way. Katie had chosen this song? And Caleb had let her? Tamera's mind flashed back to a time when she and Caleb had danced to it at a nightclub, and she'd jokingly suggested it would make a great first dance. Had Caleb told Katie about that conversation? Is that why she'd chosen the song?

The betrayals just kept on coming. It would take a miracle to escape tonight without exploding. Or crying. That might actually be worse. The hashtags practically wrote themselves.

An acoustic guitar swelled through the speakers as Katie and Caleb clung to each other, his hand uncomfortably low on her waist. The couple turned in a slow circle and Katie caught Tamera's eyes. The corners of her mouth curled up in a smirk as she pulled Caleb closer and placed a sultry kiss below his earlobe.

Was this another layer of payback for Tamera going to junior prom with Katie's high school crush? She hadn't even known Katie liked him until after the dance. The sisters had always been competitive, but things had turned vicious after that one event.

Well, Tamera was done. Her fingers curled around the flute of the champagne glass. *You won, little sis. Enjoy your spoils.* Not that Caleb was much of a catch.

"Hey." Drew snapped his fingers, and Tamera tore her gaze from the dance floor. "Stop obsessing. You're over him, remember?"

"Totally over him." That's what she kept telling everyone, at least. Tamera took a deep, shuddering breath. Thanks to her inability to keep it together in diary room interviews, pretty much all of America knew about the Katie and Caleb betrayal. The network had taken her confessions and run with them, making it a plot point throughout the entire season. How could they not, considering the engagement had, in a roundabout way, gotten Tamera cast on the show?

"Good," Drew said. "Now smile for the cameras. You never know what will end up posted online."

He was right. As a pro athlete, Drew was accustomed to the constant attention. Tamera was still getting used to it.

It was after midnight when the DJ announced the bouquet toss. Drew gripped Tamera's hand and gave her a meaningful look. "You don't have to go over there."

Tamera glanced at her mother, who stood off to the side of the dance floor with stress lines permanently etched into her brow.

"It'll make everything worse if I don't." Her mother would probably cry about how her only children were constantly at odds. The wedding guests would talk. Someone might tweet a snarky comment that would end up going viral. Pass. She was tired of being an internet meme.

Drew nodded and released her hand. "Then chin up, soldier."

She dropped a peck on his cheek. "Thanks."

Tamera walked stiffly to the dance floor, hanging out near the back of the pack of tipsy females. Caleb helped Katie onto a raised platform, his hand lingering at her waist. Bile burned Tamera's throat, but she couldn't look away from the scene. Katie's white silk dress hugged her trim figure, plunging almost as low in the front as it did in the back. Her dark chocolate hair was the same color as Tamera's, her petite stature and high cheekbones nearly identical. She caught Tamera's eye and gave a dazzling cherry red smile—one intended for the entire room. But her eyes glinted with a challenge.

"Ready?" Katie asked.

She wouldn't dare. Tamera kept her arms to her side, the fake smile she'd sported since early that morning making her cheeks ache.

Katie turned around and counted. "One... Two... Three!"

The bouquet arched through the air, and the lavender flowers plummeted right toward Tamera's head. Disbelief warred with fury as she instinctively reached out, catching the bouquet in one hand.

Cheers erupted from the wedding guests. One of the bridesmaids clutched Tamera's arm, giggling.

"You caught it!" she exclaimed.

Tamera stared at the bouquet, stunned. She heard a squeal from the stage—Katie.

What. A. Troll. Tamera imagined holding Katie down and forcing her to eat the stupid flowers while the wedding guests cheered.

A flash brought Tamera back to reality, and she blinked. The photographer dragged her toward Katie while Caleb stood nearby. His hands were shoved in his pockets, and he gave Tamera her favorite lopsided grin while his eyes roved over her figure. So gross.

Why did her heart still ache at the sight of him?

"Let's get a picture of you two with the bouquet," the photographer said, motioning for the sisters to stand next to each other.

Katie's arm snaked around Tamera's waist. "I'm so glad you caught it," she said, her voice sickly sweet. "No one deserves this more."

Tamera's smile froze on her lips, her jaw clenched tight as she fought the urge to rip the veil right off Katie's head. The last time she'd felt this angry, she'd gotten drunk while at a football game with billionaire Luke Ryder and started a fight with frat boys. That was the first time she'd become an internet sensation. She didn't want a repeat experience.

The photographer snapped a few pictures, then lowered the camera. "Now let's get the groom in there."

Caleb stepped forward and took his spot on the other side of Tamera. She could smell his cologne, feel the heat of his body. He looked so good, with his shirt sleeves rolled up to reveal the skull and crossbones tattoo that was the logo for his rock band. Her pulse beat rapidly, echoing in her ears.

"A little closer," the photographer said.

Caleb took another step, and Tamera tensed. Why had he rested his hand on the small of her back? A thousand memories assaulted her, more blinding than the camera's flash.

His hand slid significantly south of her back. Tamera let out a gasp and jumped forward.

The photographer lowered her camera. "We're good here."

They most definitely were not. Tamera stared at Caleb. His short beard emphasized the lines of his jaw, hiding the dimple she knew lay underneath. He avoided her gaze and wandered off to talk to the best man.

Katie pulled Tamera into a tight hug. "I do hope you can be happy for us."

Tamera was all too aware of the cameras snapping away. A guest even *awww*ed at the display of sisterly affection. If they only knew.

Had Caleb seriously just felt her up? For the past year, there'd been nothing but radio silence from him. He'd ignored her at every engagement soiree, family dinner, and bridal party meet-and-greet. And now, on his wedding day, he wanted to get fresh?

She hated him more in that moment than she'd thought possible. What Tamera wouldn't give for a time machine. She'd go back to the night she and Katie met Caleb, and let her sister have him then and there. They'd both been smitten by the bad boy with a leather jacket and guyliner. But at the end of the night, he'd asked for Tamera's number.

She should tell Katie what had just happened. Tamera stared at her sister, for a moment remembering her as an eight-year-old with pigtails and a Barbie obsession. They'd fought constantly about who got the Cinderella Barbie, but at the end of the day they'd loved each other.

"I guess Caleb had to date you to realize what he really wanted was me," Katie said, that sickly sweet smile still on her lips. "I'm so glad it all worked out in the end."

Ice filled Tamera's veins. "You two are perfect for each other."

Katie smiled, raising her voice so the guests could overhear. "We really are."

Tamera shoved the bouquet at Katie. "You should keep this."

"I want you to have it. So you'll always remember this day."

Tamera's hand tightened around the flower stems. Like she could ever forget.

"Time for the garter toss, Katie," the wedding planner said.

Tamera walked off the dance floor, spotting Drew immediately. He towered nearly a head above most of the wedding guests, and his muscled build was hard to miss.

Drew rested a hand at her waist and muttered some words that most certainly weren't wedding appropriate. Tamera watched as Katie sank into the chair that had been placed in the middle of the dance floor. Caleb knelt in front of her, and Katie's shrill giggles pierced the air.

Tamera was going to hurl. She turned her face into Drew's chest, trying to block out where Caleb's fingers were. The wedding guests hooted and hollered, and Katie's giggles grew louder.

Tamera pushed away from Drew, fighting the urge to cover her ears with both hands. She walked toward the ballroom exit on unsteady legs, her nails digging into the tender stems of the flowers. So what if this ended up on social media? She'd officially reached her limit. Better a photo of her leaving the party early than one of her crying.

The ballroom doors swung closed, blocking out the noise of the reception. Drew's hand caught hers and pulled her to a halt. "Hey."

She buried her face in his chest, unable to stop a few tears from leaking out onto his white shirt.

His arms trapped her to him. "Let me take you to my place."

That stopped the tears. Drew was rich, attractive, famous, and funny. But she was done with relationships.

She disentangled herself from his arms, putting some distance between them. "Thanks for being my date tonight, Drew. I couldn't have done it alone."

He tucked a strand of hair behind her ear, trying to catch her gaze. "You know I'm here for you. I've got your back, in and outside the *Eye in the Sky* house."

She nodded, quickly brushing aside a tear before it could fall. "Thank you. But I think I need to be alone tonight."

"It's your last night in Texas."

"I know, but I wouldn't be very good company."

That familiar frustrated glint echoed in his eyes, but he nodded and pulled her into a hug. "It was good seeing you again."

"Call me next time you're in L.A.," Tamera said.

Drew nodded and kissed her cheek. "Don't be a stranger." Then he strode out the front door. She knew he'd find someone else to spend the evening with in no time.

Alone in her hotel room, Tamera flung the bouquet onto a cluttered desk. It caught the edge of a file folder and knocked it to the floor, spilling across the carpet pages of house listings she'd combed through for clients. She struggled to reach the zipper on her dress, then yanked, snagging the fabric and leaving a two-inch hole. Good.

Ten minutes later, she was on a treadmill in the hotel gym, running for all she was worth. A crystal-studded bobby pin lost its grip on a curl and bounced to the floor. She ran faster, rock music pounding through her earbuds in a pathetic attempt to drown out her thoughts. Ten miles flew by as she ran until her legs felt limper than cooked noodles.

Katie could have Caleb. Instead of being Caleb's wife, Tamera would become an award-winning actress—the kind that was married to her career. Thanks to her time on *Eye in the Sky*, she'd recently signed with a talent agent. Next week, she had an audition for a minor part in a movie.

Take that, Caleb.

Tamera blinked, her eyelashes sticking together as her mascara clumped with sweat. How was Caleb now her brother-in-law? His children would be her nieces and nephews, not her sons and daughters. She'd be forced to relive the greatest heartbreak of her life at every family get-together for the rest of her life.

A sob tore from her throat, and she stumbled before regaining her footing. Crystal-studded bobby pins clung to the ends of her curls and littered the floor. Sweat coated her body and her lungs burned with exertion.

A flash of white caught the corner of Tamera's eye and she glanced to the right, expecting to see a forgotten towel hanging from the free weights. A man stared back at her, his white T-shirt stretched across taut muscles.

Tamera jumped into the air with a scream. Shaky legs reconnected with the treadmill and collapsed. Her butt slammed against the still-moving conveyor belt, and she slid backward before being dumped unceremoniously on the hard floor.

Her heart pounded furiously in her chest while she gasped for air. The man rushed forward and crouched down beside her. He still towered over her, easily over six feet tall. Cappuccino-colored hair stood on end, as though he'd recently been sleeping. Dark eyes stared at her with startling intensity from a deeply tanned face.

"Are you okay?" he asked, his face lined with concern.

Holy crap. She knew who he was.

"You're Wyatt James." Her words tumbled over themselves in uneven gasps.

"Uh, yeah." The smile vanished from his face, but he extended a hand.

She must smell worse than a football locker room right now. Tamera accepted the help up, all too aware of her sweaty skin and tear-streaked face. How humiliating.

His fingers closed around hers, and her breath hitched. His grip was strong and sure as he pulled her to her feet. The genuine concern in his eyes had her limbs turning liquid. Or maybe that was the ten miles she'd just ran.

"You're okay then?"

She grabbed a tissue from the box on the windowsill and quickly wiped her nose, sniffing. "My ego got the worst of it."

The concern in his soulful brown eyes almost made her lose it again. "Bad night?"

She laughed, fighting the urge to cover her face with both hands and sob. "That's the understatement of the century."

"Geez, I'm sorry. I hope I didn't make it worse by scaring you. I thought the gym would be empty by three a.m." He hopped onto the treadmill, but started it at a walking pace.

"You didn't make it worse." Tamera forced her rubbery legs to support her weight and got back on her own still-moving treadmill, setting it at a walking pace as well. She couldn't believe she'd been caught crying by Wyatt James, the star offensive lineman of the San Antonio Vigilantes.

He glanced at her again, his brow furrowed in concern. "Are you sure everything's okay?"

Tears burned her eyes once more, and she blinked quickly. When she spoke again, her voice was a little shaky. "My sister got married today."

"Oh." His muscled arms swung gently as he walked, and his brown eyes asked the unspoken question.

"To my ex-boyfriend."

"Oh. Oh!" He ran a hand over his closely-cropped hair. "Wow. I'm really sorry."

"Me too." She waved a hand rapidly in front of her face, trying to combat the tears. "It's kind of ironic I ran into you, since I just sent one of your teammates home. Drew was nice enough to be my date tonight."

Silence filled the room. Tamera glanced over at Wyatt, wondering if he hadn't heard her over the whir of the treadmill belts.

"How do you know Drew?" His tone was flat, all the warmth from before gone.

She blinked. Was she imagining his cold attitude? "We were both on *Eye in the Sky.*"

"The reality show. Right." Wyatt increased the pace on the treadmill, keeping his focus straight ahead.

"I'm surprised to run into you at a hotel. Don't you have a house here in San Antonio?" Drew owned a palatial mansion worth seven figures, and she assumed Wyatt probably had the same. Tamera and her business partner, Landon, had been trying to break into the high-end real estate market for almost a year. The commission from a single sale would allow her to spend months focusing only on auditions.

"They're doing some renovations on it. I'm at a hotel for a night or two."

Didn't he have a teammate who would let him crash on the couch? She opened her mouth to ask, but he'd pulled out his earbuds and placed one in his ear, the other dangling down near his massive shoulder.

He wanted to run alone. She could relate to exhaustion over fan questions. Her calf was starting to cramp anyway, and she had to leave for the airport in three hours.

"I'd better go," Tamera said, surprised at how much she wanted to stick around.

His shoulders relaxed and he nodded. "I hope you have a better day tomorrow."

"Thanks." She turned off her treadmill and picked up her phone, running a finger over the case. Her agent's voice practically screamed at her to get a picture before leaving. Right now, her biggest asset was her social media presence, and celebrity encounters were the type of photos that got lots of engagement. "Can I get a picture with you before I leave? My followers will love it."

Wyatt looked uncomfortable, but stepped off the treadmill, leaving it running. "Sure."

She grinned and opened up the app. Wyatt stood next to her, his body posture stiff. She could feel the energy coming off him in waves, and it made her entire body tingle.

Maybe she shouldn't have asked him for the photo. Yeah, her agent would be ticked if he found out, but she'd clearly made Wyatt uncomfortable. Tamera knew what it felt like to wonder if she could force a smile one more time. Oh well. It'd be awkward to take it back now. Instead, she held out her phone and positioned them in the frame. "Smile."

His entire face transformed, and she instantly recognized the "fan face" she'd seen in pictures online. She had that face, too. Landon pointed it out to her when she returned from *Eye in the Sky*.

After a few clicks she dropped her phone, and Wyatt immediately stepped away. Cool air rushed in to brush her skin where his had almost touched hers moments before.

"Good luck on the upcoming season," Tamera said, trying to act unaffected by his presence.

"Thanks. It was nice to meet you."

"You, too."

Wyatt tucked both buds into his ears and increased the speed on the treadmill. Tamera stood in the doorway, admiring his long and even stride, before shaking her head and leaving. She pulled out her phone, fingers flying as she posted the best of the five photos to social media. *Met Wyatt James tonight!* she posted. *#celebritysighting #footballforever*

Within seconds, she had over fifty likes and a few comments. And for the first time, the weekend didn't seem like a total loss.

Chapter Two

Wyatt glanced over his shoulder to make sure Tamera had really left. The door to the hotel gym was tightly closed, and all signs of the sorrowful brunette were gone.

He breathed a sigh of relief. His protective instincts had kicked in when he saw her tears, but then she'd mentioned Drew and asked for a photo. After the disastrous last five months—thanks for that, Drew—Wyatt just wanted to run in a hotel gym without having his picture plastered across social media. He'd get enough unwanted press after tomorrow.

She'd looked so devastated, with her eyes rimmed in makeup and skin splotchy from crying. He'd wanted to tuck her in his arms and promise her everything would be okay. That would've been a very bad idea, considering he'd sworn off women for good.

Wyatt rolled his shoulders, then increased the speed on the treadmill. Time to put Tamera's enticing hazel eyes out of his head and focus on plotting a satisfying third act for his latest script. He'd rediscovered his love of writing since Becky left.

Scratch that. Since Drew *stole* Becky, blamed a career-damaging injury on Wyatt, and got him transferred to the floundering Los Angeles Coyotes.

Tamera would make a great character in a script. She had managed to look both adorable and broken while sitting on the ground in a heap, mouth opened in a surprised *o*. Her skin glistened with perspiration. A pink tank top clung to her body, wet with exertion. Her espresso-colored hair was a mess of frizzy curls. But in that moment, he'd never found a woman more attractive. Then he'd caught sight of the tears, and everything in him demanded he fix whatever was wrong.

Yeah right. He couldn't even fix his own problems, let alone a woman's. Especially not a woman who was friends with Drew.

The script. That's what he should focus on. It'd distract him from how much he was dreading tomorrow, when he'd officially become a resident of California.

He managed to spend all of two minutes contemplating how to get his hero and heroine out of the morgue without alerting the bad guys before something sparkled near the floor, drawing his attention. The carpet around Tamera's vacant treadmill was littered with fancy clips that glittered in the fluorescent lighting, silently taunting him with their presence. Had Drew really been her date for her sister and ex-boyfriend's wedding? There had to be a story there.

"Stop it," he growled aloud.

He was moving to California tomorrow. Somehow, he had to figure out how to start over. No more cheating girlfriends. No more playing for his dream team—the one he'd drooled over and cheered for since he was six years old. No more soft southern drawls and gun racks mounted on every truck.

Tomorrow was where his focus should be. Not on some girl who he'd had a five-minute conversation with.

He shook his head as anger tried to strangle him. Drew hadn't even stuck with Becky a month before casting her aside—shortly after the shoulder injury that was supposedly Wyatt's fault, in fact. Part of Wyatt thought his ex deserved it, but another part of him ached that she'd thrown away their six-month relationship for a fling. He'd been daydreaming about their future together, and she'd been sneaking off with the quarterback.

Wyatt ran ten miles, managing to maintain just over a six-minute pace. By the time he showered and collapsed into bed, it was almost five in the morning. Still, he couldn't manage to relax and fall asleep. Worry about the upcoming press conference niggled at the back of his mind. His entire chest tightened at the mere thought of being on television, but the Q and A with reporters was standard protocol after a trade. The speculation over his switch from the Vigilantes, who were favored to win the championships this year, to the Coyotes, who barely made it to the playoffs most seasons, would run rampant. And Wyatt couldn't do a thing about it.

He still wasn't sure how Drew had managed to spin his injury as Wyatt's fault to the coach. Drew claimed Wyatt intentionally let him get sacked as revenge for the Becky situation, and Coach had believed him. Nothing Wyatt did or said could convince him otherwise. Drew told Wyatt if he didn't agree to the trade, he'd tell the press it was all Wyatt's fault. That's what he got for going up against the darling of the Vigilantes—defeated.

Were Tamera and Drew close friends, or just acquaintances? Did she know what he'd done to Wyatt?

With a sigh, Wyatt grabbed his tablet and pulled up Tamera's bio from the show website. Might as well satisfy his curiosity since sleep clearly wasn't going to happen. The bio was short, but enlightening. Tamera had grown up in a military family and moved frequently before finally graduating from high school in Texas, which explained why her sister had gotten married here. She was naturally competitive and loved watching and playing all types of sports, although football was her favorite. Another reason she was friends with Drew?

Wyatt's phone buzzed, pulling his attention from the webpage.

You awake? Shows you're online.

Seriously, did Bobby ever sleep? His agent was probably still wearing his suit from yesterday, hunched over a laptop in his sparsely decorated home office with a string of licorice in one hand and cold coffee nearby.

I'm up. Wyatt had barely pushed send when his phone started ringing.

"It's five in the morning," Wyatt said. "Are you just waking up or going to bed?"

"I'll sleep after the press conference." Bobby's tone was breezy, like staying up for twenty-four hours straight was no big deal. "That's actually why I called. Mr. Ryder wants to move it up an hour. Something came up, and he really wants to be there for his first trade since buying the team. It would mean coming straight from the airport."

Wyatt's chest tightened again with nerves, and he took a slow breath. This was okay. Good, even. Less time to anticipate the torture of sitting in front of dozens of microphones while cameras filmed his every move. "That's fine."

"Good, because I already told him to move up the time. No sense angering the new boss."

Wyatt rolled his eyes and clicked on an article of Tamera. "So glad you asked."

"This is probably the last trade of your career." Bobby's tone was suddenly serious. "You'll be lucky to play another five years. Might as well make it count."

Five years. The looming deadline felt worse than a shoulder to the gut. Football had been Wyatt's entire life for so long. But the whispered accusations from Drew had made Wyatt realize just how quickly his career could end, whether it was by injury or by damage to his reputation. Or just by age. What was he supposed to do once football was no longer an option?

Wyatt glanced at the script open on his laptop. But that was a hobby, not a career. "I'm making the best of this, Bobby."

"Good." Bobby's voice was gruff. "I know it's not what you wanted, but word on the street is you aren't the only trade for the Coyotes. You might still have a shot at a championship-winning season. I think McKinley will be good for the team."

Wyatt wasn't holding his breath over that one. McKinley had recently been hired as the coach, but the Coyotes would have to trade half the team for a decent shot at the championship. "Guess we'll find out."

"Stop being so pessimistic. Mr. Ryder's invited you to dinner after the press conference. McKinley will be there, too. I accepted the invitation on your behalf."

"Whoa." Wyatt dropped the tablet to his bed and leaned forward. He'd never been invited to an owner's house before, and the Coyotes would be his third team since being drafted. Had Drew gone back on his word and passed along an anonymous tip? Wyatt struggled to control his breathing. He'd watched the replay of Drew's injury dozens of times. Wyatt had left Drew open to being taken down by the other team. But that had been a miscalculation on Wyatt's part, not a deliberate attempt at sabotage, which is exactly how the sportscasters had interpreted things in the playback.

Drew had told Wyatt if he didn't take the trade, he'd go public with his version of the truth. And Drew's version unfortunately sounded all too believable—and cast Wyatt in a very bad light.

"I'm sure they just want to get to know you better," Bobby said. "Mr. Ryder seems like a very hands-on owner."

"Guess we'll find out. Can you make sure I have somewhere to change clothes and freshen up before the conference?"

"Already got a hotel room booked nearby. Don't worry—I made sure it was a piece of crap so you aren't wasting any of your precious money."

Wyatt rolled his eyes and looked around his current hotel room. Bobby acted like a decent economy hotel was akin to a third-world country. But the last few months had changed a lot of things for Wyatt, and how he handled money was one of them. He wasn't going to make the same mistake as other professional athletes and be broke by thirty. "See you tomorrow. I'd better get some sleep before I leave for the airport in a few hours."

"Don't be late," Bobby said, and hung up without saying goodbye.

Dinner with the owner and head coach. Surely Drew hadn't told Mr. Ryder anything. It would've put the trade in jeopardy, and Wyatt staying in Texas was the last thing Drew wanted.

Wyatt shook his head and returned to the article on his tablet. It was no use obsessing over the reason for dinner. He'd find out soon enough.

The *Eye in the Sky* website mentioned both Drew and Tamera frequently in the articles about last season. She had won a record seven Head Honcho competitions while on the show. A good thing, too, or she surely would've been voted out by the other players long before the final four—at least that's what the message boards claimed. Wyatt opened a new tab and input Tamera's name into the web browser. A slew of online celebrity gossip magazines and blogs showed up. But one name stood out to him—Luke Ryder.

Wyatt frowned and clicked on the link. What connection did Tamera have to the owner of the Los Angeles Coyotes?

The article was almost a year and a half old. Wyatt's eyes widened at the headline—*Toujour date major disaster for Billionaire playboy.* Toujour... He wracked his brain for a connection. That's right. Toujour was a professional matchmaking firm that Luke's wife ran. Tamera had been a Toujour client? What's more, she'd dated Luke Ryder?

Why did that make Wyatt so uncomfortable?

He clicked on the video and watched as an obviously inebriated Tamera spilled beer all over Luke while lunging at the three big guys in the row behind her. She'd seemed emotional tonight, but not like the type to get drunk and flip out. Then again, you couldn't know a person in five minutes. This wasted version of Tamera definitely seemed like Drew's type. After dumping Becky, the quarterback had probably been on the lookout for his next conquest.

Wyatt clicked on a link at the bottom of the article and watched an interview Tamera had done while on *Eye in the Sky.*

"Yeah, I freaked out a little on that date," she said, flashing the camera a winning smile. "Not my finest moment, obviously. But I'd just found out my sister and ex-boyfriend were engaged, and she asked me to be the maid of honor. They had an affair behind my back for an entire year. How would you react?"

Wyatt's breakup with Becky hadn't been quite that dramatic, but he definitely hadn't reacted well. His distraction on the field, and resulting trade to the Coyotes, was evidence of that.

"Yeah, I'm still mad," Tamera said as the interview continued. "How's that going to affect my game play? I'm going to channel my anger into the competitions and kick butt."

Wyatt couldn't help but smile at that.

"When I win that million dollars, I'm going to buy Katie and Caleb a very nice wedding present," Tamera told the camera. "After all, if not for their betrayal, I wouldn't be here."

Wyatt laughed out loud. Tamera had spunk. He could see why America loved her. She had entire pages dedicated to her on social media, and it seemed fans had practically rioted when she came in fourth place instead of first.

He'd sworn to never watch *Eye in the Sky* since Drew was on it. But something about Tamera begged him to find out more.

Wyatt clicked on the first episode, paid the fee, and started watching. He could sleep on the plane.

Chapter Three

⟋⟋⟋

The plane pulled to a stop and a *ding* sounded throughout the cabin as the fasten seatbelt sign flickered off. Tamera breathed a sigh of relief as she gathered her purse. The flight had been long, filled with restless sleep that was almost worse than none at all. Right now, all she wanted was to forget this weekend had ever happened.

You're lying, her mind whispered, conjuring a picture of Wyatt in his loose white shirt and navy blue gym shorts. His eyes had to be the kindest she'd ever stared into. No man had ever crouched down beside her and asked if she was okay.

Whatever. Wyatt had been nice, but she was unlikely to ever see him again. Unless Drew held some sort of team party and invited her to it...

No. She lived in Los Angeles, and flying to San Antonio for a party she may or may not see Wyatt at would be beyond ridiculous.

She fished her phone from her purse and switched off airplane mode. Notifications flashed across the screen, three hours of suppressed interactions bursting forth. She clicked on the first one and grinned. Nearly a thousand comments on her photo with Wyatt already, and more than ten thousand likes. That should make her agent happy. Maybe it would even impress a casting director, like the one she was auditioning for in a few days. The part wasn't big—just a minor role as a waitress—but it was a step above being an extra, and it was a big-name Hollywood film.

She read a few of the photo comments, content to wait in her window seat while the other passengers fought to get off the plane. It seemed every other comment was someone swooning over Wyatt. Yes, he most definitely was insanely attractive with that square jaw and almost military-short dark brown hair. The five o'clock shadow and bulging biceps did make him look like a hero in an action film.

I see Drew's making sure you meet the team! someone had commented. *Make sure to keep posting pictures. #yummy*

Fifty-nine replies to that one comment. Tamera scrolled through them and couldn't help rolling her eyes.

You should be ashamed of yourself! Drew got you to top four on EITS and now you're snuggling up with his teammate?

Are you and Wyatt a thing now???

Does this mean #tampsey is over?

Tampsey had been the ridiculous celebrity couple name used for Tamera and Drew on *Eye in the Sky*—a meshing of her first name and his last name, Dempsey. Fans just couldn't seem to accept that the two of them would only ever be just friends.

She typed out a comment, reiterating that she and Drew were just friends and that she'd barely met Wyatt and was therefore not dating him, but deleted it before posting. It wouldn't matter anyway.

The seats were slowly emptying around her as the line of weary passengers moved forward. Tamera grabbed her purse and hooked it over one shoulder, then clicked over to the next notification on her screen.

A photo stared up at her, the bright white and pale lavender of the silk dresses standing out against the poorly lit ballroom. Katie clutched Tamera close, the bouquet of flowers squished between them.

Tamera lurched forward and her purse tumbled to the floor. She quickly grabbed it and stepped into the aisle, her eyes glued to the phone. She'd known it was likely someone would post a photo of last night and tag her, but did it have to be this one?

The line moved slowly forward and Tamera shuffled toward the front of the plane, sandwiched between a businessman in a suit and a mother holding a fussy baby. The photo, posted by an old high school friend Tamera hadn't spoken to in years, had no caption. But the album was public, and Tamera had been tagged. The post had over six thousand reactions, ranging from the angry face to the heart. Katie looked so smug in the photo, like she held the world in her hands. Tamera's shock was forever immortalized. The flash from the camera had washed out her complexion, highlighting a smile that looked more like a grimace.

They were on their honeymoon now. Tamera tried to block out the image of Caleb and Katie rolling around in the white sands of the Bahamas, their hands everywhere. That had been Tamera's dream honeymoon destination, once upon a time. Now it was forever ruined.

Something yanked at her hair, making Tamera's scalp sting uncomfortably and pulling her back to the present.

"I'm so sorry," the mother said from behind, grabbing her son's hand and disentangling it from Tamera's hair.

"No worries."

The mother stared, a smile lighting up her face. "Oh my gosh! Tamera Hadley. I loved you on *Eye in the Sky*."

A fan. Tamera could almost feel herself transforming into the star this woman wanted her to be. Her smile grew so wide it was almost physically painful, and she straightened her posture and put a happy lilt into her voice. "You are too sweet. It's so nice to meet you. What did you say your name was?"

"Anna." The woman grabbed her son's hand just before it caught another lock of Tamera's hair. "I felt so awful for you. My sister stole a boyfriend from me, too. In high school, so they didn't end up getting married, but still. I was a wreck. Did your sister and ex end up going through with the wedding? I kept hoping they'd break things off."

Tamera's smile tightened. "Yes, they did. That's where I'm coming back from, actually."

The woman's face darkened in a scowl. "What a snake. You're better off without him. You'll find someone better soon."

"You're sweet to say so." Except that Tamera was most definitely done with relationships.

"Did you and Drew really not have a showmance? It looked so real on TV, but I've seen the interviews where you say you weren't together."

"Drew's a dear friend—and only a friend." Tamera took a few steps forward, closing the gap between her and the businessman in front of her. She could see the plane's open door, now only a few feet away. "Well, I hope you have a wonderful day. It was so nice to meet you."

"You too," the woman said.

Tamera hurried up the gangway and sucked in the cool air of the airport terminal. Soon everyone would know the wedding had really happened. Should Tamera ignore it and hope everyone stopped gossiping? Thank her followers for their support in a live video? Post her own photos of the wedding and act like she was totally fine?

Tears stung her eyes, but she refused to let them fall. Katie didn't deserve Tamera's sympathy, and Caleb certainly wasn't worth it.

Three hours later, she was finally home and unpacked. Tamera sank onto her living room couch and flipped on the television. She had about five hours of shows to catch up on after her weekend away, and now felt like the perfect time to focus on mindless entertainment. She kicked up her feet on the coffee table and selected a police procedural. The detective had just been called to the scene of the crime when her phone buzzed. She picked it up and grinned at Drew's name. They'd started out as allies in the house, but now she considered him a real friend.

You met Wyatt and didn't tell me??

It was like three in the morning. Crazy, huh?

Her phone buzzed again, but this time it was a text from her real estate partner, Landon, asking if they could meet tomorrow morning to go over the newest listings. She quickly agreed. He'd happily taken over all her clients while she was on *Eye in the Sky*. Now she was trying her best to return the favor while he helped his wife through a difficult pregnancy. They finalized plans, and then Tamera opened up Drew's new text.

Be careful. Wyatt isn't what he seems.

Tamera stared at the text, re-reading the words. **What does that mean???**

Just trust me, okay?

Trust him. Tamera laughed out loud, the sound echoing back to her in the empty condo. Caleb had effectively killed her ability to trust. In the end, her suspicions and paranoia had gotten her sent home from *Eye in the Sky*.

Another text came through. **I always had your back on EITS, didn't I?**

Tamera chewed on her lip. Drew had looked out for her on the show, but she knew from watching the season that he'd also spent a lot of time looking out for himself. She had no doubt that he would've thrown her under the bus in a second if it had furthered his game.

That's the show, she reminded herself. At the end of the day, they'd all been playing for themselves. That didn't mean the friendships she'd formed in the house weren't real.

It was just a fun pic to get some engagement from fans. Gotta keep my agent happy.

Be careful, Drew repeated.

She rolled her eyes. Man, he could be cryptic when he wanted to be. She'd hated that about him while in the house.

Thanks for the warning, Mom. I'll be so careful that I'll probably never see him again.

She clicked over to social media. The comments on her photo of Wyatt continued to grow by the second. The comments on the picture of her and Katie were doing the same, but she tried to ignore those notifications as much as possible.

Katie and Caleb were probably sipping Mai Tais in a private cabana right now. His swimming suit would hang low on his hips, his chest covered in sand—

She took a shuddering breath. Time to think about something else. Anything else. Notifications kept buzzing, alerting her to new comments on the Wyatt photo.

Look at those abs! #smokinghot

You look amazing, Tamera! Where did you get that cute tank?

Is Wyatt moving to California for you???

Tamera laughed out loud while the television droned on in the background. She'd probably have to rewatch this episode, because she wasn't paying very good attention to the show. But seriously. What had made that obviously insane fan think Wyatt was moving to California?

She posted a link to the boutique where she'd bought her exercise gear, then kept scrolling.

Is #tampsey officially over? #tameratt #forever

Tameratt. Good thing that she and Wyatt weren't a couple, because that was even worse than Tampsey.

*You stole my favorite player from my favorite team, Tamera!!! *sob**

Can't believe Wyatt James has been traded to the Coyotes. Unreal!

Wait. What?

Tamera gasped at the comments that continued to fill her feed. Wyatt had really been traded to the Coyotes? She quickly clicked on the search bar, but didn't have to look very far for proof. *Wyatt James traded to the Los Angeles Coyotes* was the top trending story in sports.

No freaking way. Tamera clicked on the first link and realized it was a live video of a press conference. Wyatt sat in the middle of a long table, flanked on his sides by Coach McKinley and Luke Ryder. It was weird seeing Wyatt and Luke sitting next to each other, like two very bizarre parts of her life had suddenly collided. Tamera hadn't been at all surprised when Luke had ended up engaged to his matchmaker not long after their date. It had been pretty obvious he was emotionally unavailable. But he'd been a good sport about her horrifyingly poor behavior that night, and had said nothing but kind things about her to the press in the weeks that followed. She'd always been grateful for that.

Wyatt tugged at his tie and leaned down to speak into the microphones spread before him. "I'm very excited to join the Los Angeles Coyotes this season." His voice was monotone, and his forehead shone under the California sun. "I can't wait to work with Coach McKinley and some of the most talented players in the league."

"You've got to be kidding. You were already working with the most talented players in the league." Tamera shook her head in disbelief. What could've possibly possessed Wyatt to accept a trade to a B-list team like the Coyotes? Sure, they had a new owner and a new coach. But you didn't turn around a team in a single season. That kind of stuff only happened in the movies.

She quickly picked up her phone and texted Drew. **Wyatt's been traded??? Did he have a concussion at the time?**

Things happened. Can't say anything else.

Tamera chewed on her lip, watching as Wyatt answered a reporter's question. His stiff posture practically screamed his discomfort. She'd watched him in a few game interviews, and he was always a little awkward in front of the camera. But this had to be more than just nerves.

The Coyotes. Seriously, he chose the Coyotes over the Vigilantes?

"What are you doing, Wyatt James?" Tamera asked his image.

She listened to the rest of the interview, but Wyatt never gave an answer.

Chapter Four

Wyatt looked across the sea of microphones and reporters, his heart beating frantically in his chest. Were his armpits sweating? Thank heaven his suit coat would hide it. He could barely remember what questions he'd answered over the past hour. Hopefully he hadn't sounded like too big of an idiot. Bobby hadn't sent any warning glares his way, which had to be a good sign.

"That's all the questions we have time for today," the team's press liaison said into the microphones. "Thank you for coming."

He'd survived. Wyatt rose and followed the others off the platform as the reporters shouted a few last questions at their retreating figures. Fans stood behind a barricade, waving signs and screaming his name. If word got out that Drew blamed Wyatt for his injury, they'd be screaming something much angrier. Drew was one of the best quarterbacks in the league, and because of that injury he'd spend half of the upcoming season on the bench.

A security guard made his way through the screaming fans, cutting a path to the limo. A tanned blonde showing too much skin thrust a pen at Wyatt.

"Sign my shirt," she begged, pointing to her chest.

Wyatt was sure his ears were bright red. His little sister, Natalie, would be doubled over from laughter if she were here.

He took the pen from the woman, careful not to let his hand touch hers, and signed her white tank on the shoulder. He handed the pen back to the woman, and she clutched at it hungrily.

Did Tamera have to deal with this when she went out in public? The thought blinked into his mind like a neon sign and wouldn't leave. Wyatt wasn't much for reality TV, but he knew that popular shows, like *Eye in the Sky*, had robust fan bases. It wasn't hard to imagine muscled men vying for Tamera's attention. Her electric smile and petite figure, with curves in all the right places, were practically magnets.

Wyatt followed closely behind the security guard, but only made it a few more feet before the bright eyes of a young boy caught his attention. The boy held out a football, waving it wildly back and forth. Wyatt couldn't resist that kind of plea. He crouched down near the child, who was perhaps five or six, and took the offered football and pen.

"What's your name?" he asked the kid.

The boy bounced up and down, grinning from ear to ear. His mother's hand landed on his shoulder in a vain attempt to calm him down.

"James," the boy said. "My daddy named me after you!"

Wyatt paused, then quickly finished signing the football as emotion clogged his throat.

"That's a good name," he said, handing the football back.

"Can we get a picture?" the mom ventured.

"Of course." Wyatt posed for the photo, then gave the boy a wave and moved on.

Maybe his career hadn't taken the trajectory he wanted, but fans weren't to blame. He'd put his best foot forward while playing for the Coyotes, and make the best of a crummy situation. Maybe Bobby was right, and the new players and coach would finally turn the team around.

For the next half hour, Wyatt signed anything thrust toward him and smiled for photos until his cheeks ached. A security guard held the door to the limousine open, waiting for Wyatt to climb inside.

"We love you!" someone yelled from the back of the crowd.

Wyatt raised his hand in a wave and gave his biggest smile. "Go Coyotes!"

A cheer rippled through the crowd. Wyatt gave one last wave, then climbed into the limo and let the door shut behind him.

Blessed peace. Wyatt let his smile drop and slumped against the rich leather seats. He'd never realized how much he craved time alone with his own thoughts until silence was a rarity.

"Great job," Bobby said from the other side of the car. Sunlight glinted off his bald head and highlighted the fine wrinkles forming around his eyes and mouth. He didn't look up from his tablet, which he furiously typed into. "Everyone's confused by the trade, but overall the early press numbers are favorable—except from Texas, of course. San Antonio isn't pleased you've left their fair city."

Wyatt wasn't exactly pleased himself. "I didn't act nervous?"

Bobby glanced up for a fraction of a second. "Fans are used to you being a little stiff off the field. It was fine."

Fine—not great. Wyatt mentally shrugged it off. He was paid to play football, not to act. "Guess that's all I can ask for."

"You're doing great, kid." Bobby dropped his tablet onto the seat beside him. "I know this isn't what you wanted, but the new players they drafted look promising. You might still get a championship ring."

Wyatt barely held back a snort. If that happened, it'd be a comeback story right out of the movies.

"Loosen up," Bobby said. "The Coyotes are paying you a lot of money to be here. Act happy about it at dinner."

"Better playing for the Coyotes than not at all, right?"

"That's the spirit."

Wyatt stretched his legs, then grabbed a bottle of water from the mini-fridge. The adrenaline of the crowds was wearing off, and he felt a little shaky. "Are we headed to dinner now?"

"Yes, at Mr. Ryder's penthouse."

Wyatt raised an eyebrow. "Not a restaurant?"

"Nope."

Okay then.

The limo fought through the snarling Los Angeles traffic as Wyatt tried to stop replaying every interaction he'd had tonight with a fan.

Had he seemed happy enough? Accessible enough? Excited enough? Lately, it seemed like whatever he did, it was never enough. Becky had certainly felt that way. Why else would she have dumped him for a tool like Drew?

Natalie would tell him if he'd looked like a dork in the press conference. Wyatt could always count on his sister to be honest.

"Stop thinking," Bobby commanded without looking up from his tablet.

Wyatt startled, but didn't comment. Somehow Bobby always knew when Wyatt was too much in his own head. So he closed his eyes and tried to think of nothing.

By the time the limo pulled up in front of the glass-fronted high-rise, he'd decompressed from the crowds of the press conference and was ready to put on his game face and officially meet the owner and coach. They'd been at the press conference, of course, but Wyatt had barely had time to exchange a handshake before the questions started.

The doorman verified their credentials, then led them into an elevator. The attendant inserted a key and selected the penthouse. Wyatt swallowed, trying not to fidget uncomfortably as soft jazz music played in the background.

The elevator pinged open, and Wyatt and Bobby stepped into a ten-by-ten entryway with twelve-foot-high ceilings. White marble flooring sparkled under the chrome and glass chandelier above them.

"Welcome. Mr. Ryder has been alerted to your arrival."

Wyatt didn't jump at the cool feminine voice that surrounded them from all sides, unsurprised by its presence. Of course Luke would have Talia, the home automation system that had made him a billionaire, in his own home.

Bobby stared at the glass-fronted double doors. "Do we knock?"

Wyatt shrugged. Before he could speak, the doors swung open.

A woman stood before them in stockinged feet and a pencil skirt. Her chestnut-colored hair with golden highlights hung around her shoulders, and her stomach held the slightest roundness underneath her silk blouse. When she smiled, her entire face lightened.

"Wyatt," Brooke said, pulling the door open wider and standing aside. "I'm so glad you could come."

"Thank you for inviting us." He stepped inside and motioned to Bobby. "You remember my agent?"

"Of course." Brooke held out a hand, and Wyatt realized that Bobby and Brooke were nearly the same height. "It's so nice to see you both again."

She motioned for them to follow her, and Wyatt stared in awe as they made their way through the house. Everything screamed wealth, from the ten-foot-tall heavy wood doors in a bright white to the plush gray carpet.

"Luke had to take a phone call, but he'll be out any minute now," Brooke said over her shoulder. "I've got Bryan in the kitchen stirring the sauce."

Bryan... Bryan... Wyatt almost laughed when he realized she was referring to Coach McKinley. He'd watched the coach, both on television and at games, and couldn't imagine him as anything but fierce. He wondered what had made McKinley join the Coyotes. Blackmail, same as Wyatt?

"You've got a beautiful home." Wyatt fought the urge to wipe his sweaty palms on his slacks. Why couldn't he be cool in social situations?

"Thanks," Brooke said. "I'm excited for the new house, but it'll be hard to leave this one."

"Oh, you're moving?"

"Yeah, construction should finish in another few months. We want our kids to grow up with lots of space to run and play."

Brooke stepped off the plush carpet of the living room and onto weathered gray barnwood. The kitchen was wide and open, with tall cabinets and lots of counter space. Wyatt barely held back a laugh when his eyes landed on McKinley. Coach had a lavender apron tied around his waist, and the ruffles at the bottom barely brushed the tops of his thighs.

Brooke smiled at McKinley. "Thank you, Bryan. I can take it from here."

"Sure I can't help you with anything else?" McKinley asked, handing the metal whisk over to Brooke.

"I've got it. You boys go socialize." She made a shooing motion. "Dinner's almost finished anyway."

Coach McKinley turned toward Wyatt, arms folded across his broad chest. He had to be close to six and a half feet tall, and his shoulders were as broad as any linebacker's.

Wyatt took a step forward and extended his hand. He cleared his throat, trying to project an outward calm. "Coach McKinley. It's an honor to officially meet you, sir."

McKinley took Wyatt's hand and pumped it up and down, his grip strong. "We're excited to have you join the Coyotes."

"I'm thrilled to be here."

"It's a new era for the team," McKinley said confidently. "We'll get you that ring before retirement, don't you worry."

Wyatt coughed in surprise. McKinley folded his arms again and kept his gaze steady.

"You'll love the guys on the team," Brooke broke in. "Bryan was kind enough to introduce us to everyone about a month ago."

Wyatt smiled blandly. Of course the guys were on their best behavior around the new owner and his wife. What happened in the locker room would give Wyatt a true feel for his new teammates. At least this time, one very important detail would be different—Wyatt wouldn't have a girlfriend for the quarterback to steal.

"The rolls have now achieved their optimal internal temperature," Talia said, her cool voice echoing throughout the kitchen. "Please remove them from the oven."

"I didn't expect to be treated to a home-cooked meal tonight." Bobby rubbed his hands together. "It smells delicious."

"Thanks. I try and keep things as normal as possible at home." Brooke set the rolls on top of the counter, then returned to briskly stirring whatever was in the pan on the stove.

"Are you sure we can't help with anything?" Wyatt asked.

She flashed him a smile. "It's sweet of you to offer, but I think I've got it. As soon as Luke is here, I'll have him pull the chicken cordon bleu and au gratin potatoes out of the oven."

Wyatt's mouth watered as the yeasty scent of the rolls filled the kitchen. He hadn't had a home-cooked meal since visiting his family over Christmas. In San Antonio, a nutritionist provided all his meals—part of his contract with the Vigilantes—but she'd never provided anything particularly tasty. Hopefully his nutritionist here would be more concerned with taste.

"Are you trying to slow Wyatt here down in the games?" McKinley asked, but his tone was light.

Brooke laughed. "One good meal won't kill either of you. Tomorrow you can go back to counting macros or whatever it is you guys do."

McKinley held up two fingers. "Two rolls, James. Fill up on the protein."

Wyatt nodded. "You've got it, Coach."

Brooke pulled the hot rolls off the pan and dropped them into a basket. Luke appeared in the kitchen then. He'd discarded his suit coat and rolled up the sleeves of his light green button-down shirt.

"Sorry about that," he said, extending a hand to both Wyatt and Bobby. "Welcome to our home. We're so glad you could come."

"It's an honor, Mr. Ryder," Wyatt said, shaking his hand.

"Please, call me Luke." He clapped Wyatt on the shoulder. "I'm so excited to have you here."

"I'm excited to be here," Wyatt lied. Something in the tone of Luke's voice made him nervous.

Luke dropped a hand to Brooke's back and leaned down, kissing her neck. She smiled, her shoulders hunching forward as though hiding a shiver. Wyatt looked away, feeling like he was intruding on a private moment. What would it be like to have such an obviously loving relationship?

You're staying single, he reminded himself. He wasn't going to let a woman ruin his career anymore than one already had.

Soon they were all sitting at the dining room table, plates piled high with the delicious scents. Wyatt took a bite of his chicken, lightly covered in the sauce Brooke had been stirring, and barely held back a groan.

"This is fantastic," he said.

Brooke's cheeks pinked and she smiled. "Thank you. My job doesn't leave a lot of time to cook, but I enjoy it when I can."

That's right. Brooke was a matchmaker at Toujour. She'd matched Tamera up with Luke. Luke, the new owner of the Coyotes. Tamera, the girl Wyatt couldn't seem to get out of his head. He was dying to ask about Tamera, but that would seem beyond weird.

"This really is a treat," McKinley agreed. Wyatt noticed that while he was only allowed two rolls, the coach had snagged three for himself.

"So, Wyatt," Luke broke in. "Did you sell your home in San Antonio? You mentioned it was on the market last time we spoke."

"I did." He'd signed the papers the day he met Tamera, in fact, which was why he'd spent the night at a hotel. Letting the home go wasn't as hard as he'd thought it would be. It felt good to rid himself of the bad Becky memories there. "I've already got a real estate agent lined up to help me look for a new place here."

"Good. We hope you'll be in California for a long time." Luke grabbed a roll and buttered it. "Did you know my dad always wanted to buy the team?"

Wyatt wiped at his mouth with a napkin. Luke's father had founded Ryder Communications and made it a household name before succumbing to lung cancer a few years earlier. "I knew he bought the Lakers, but didn't realize he liked football, too."

"Even more than basketball probably."

Brooke reached across the table and grasped Luke's hand, giving him a smile so full of love it made Wyatt's insides ache. "Luke was so excited when the chance to buy the team came up."

Wyatt nodded, not sure what he was supposed to say. Where was this going?

"It's not exactly a secret that the Coyotes have struggled the past few years," Luke continued.

"Not anymore." McKinley brushed roll crumbs off his graying mustache. "We've got some good new recruits, and Schroeder's a decent enough quarterback when his ego doesn't get in the way. You're joining a brand new team, Wyatt."

"One that's going to win the championship," Luke cut in. "Ticket sales have suffered the last few years because the team hasn't performed well. And because there aren't fans cheering them on from the stands, the team's morale suffers and they play even poorer."

"It's a vicious cycle," McKinley agreed. "A stadium's energy can make or break a game."

"Which means it's time to rally fan support." Luke leveled a gaze at Wyatt. "You're the start of that."

Wyatt's stomach felt like a football had just been inflated inside it. The food soured in his mouth, and he set down his fork. "I'm not sure I understand."

"You're new blood," Luke said. "The fans have already lost faith in most of our existing players, and the new recruits don't have any public support yet. But when news broke of your trade, the internet practically danced."

Wyatt tried not to let his panic show. He didn't want attention. He wanted to lay low.

Luke leaned forward, staring at Wyatt across the table. "The press conference today has already gotten a really positive response. We want to capitalize on that by running a few different television commercials and print ads. Really get people excited to see you play this season. The PR department thinks it'll drive ticket sales."

It was a good thing Wyatt didn't have food in his mouth right then, because he would've choked. "You want me to do a TV commercial?"

Bobby shot Wyatt a warning look. "This is great news. Wyatt's an excellent choice."

Of course Bobby was happy about this. Per Wyatt's contract with the Coyotes, the additional promotion would pad his paycheck nicely— and, by extension, Bobby's.

"I'm not exactly great in front of the camera," Wyatt admitted. He knew the excuse was lame even as it left his mouth. He'd seen himself in interviews, and *stiff* was a nice way of putting things. The effortless way Tamera had handled the camera on *Eye in the Sky* was an impossibility for someone like him.

Luke waved a hand dismissively. "We can work with that."

Wyatt doubted very much an acting coach—even one as talented as Tamera—would help. But only an idiot would refuse a direct request from the team owner. So Wyatt forced himself to speak through his tight throat.

"Okay then. I'm in."

Chapter Five

Tamera looked around the crowded room of thin women with perky chests and California suntans, suddenly feeling very unsure of herself. She tightened her grip on her purse strap as her heartbeat quickened. There had to be twenty women in here, all as eager to be cast in the role as she was.

A woman with perfect blonde beach waves glared at Tamera, like her presence in the room was a personal insult. Tamera dropped her hand from the purse strap and raised her chin. She might never have been cast in a movie, but she *had* been cast on a reality television show and made it to the top four. That had to count for something. She belonged here as much as any of these women.

She checked in at the metal desk manned by a cranky grandma with a silver beehive hairdo, then took an empty seat near the door that she assumed led to the audition room. Time to harness the negative energy and turn it into something positive, just like she had on *Eye in the Sky*. She closed her eyes and took a deep breath, imagining how good it would feel to win when everyone was rooting for her to fail.

Her phone vibrated in her purse, and she pulled it out to find a text from Drew.

Good luck.

Thanks. I'm so nervous!

Did you even see yourself on EITS? You'll do great.

Tamera had seen herself on *Eye in the Sky*—had watched the entire season as soon as she got home after the finale. It was hard to view herself objectively. The diary room interviews where she cried about Caleb and Katie were particularly excruciating to watch. Drew's scheming—and the realization he'd throw her under the bus to save his own game—hadn't been easy to see, either. But whatever. That was the game, and Drew was proving to be a pretty good friend outside of the *Eye in the Sky* house.

"Tamera Hadley."

It was go time. An image flashed unexpectedly into her mind of Wyatt crouched beside her on the gym floor, asking if she was okay. His quiet, comforting presence would be nice right about now.

Ridiculous. She shoved her phone back in her purse and followed the thin boy who had to be an intern—was he even out of high school yet?—through the magical door that turned unknown actors and actresses into household names.

"Good luck," he said in a flat monotone before closing the door behind her.

She bit back the words on the tip of her tongue—a very sarcastic *thanks for the encouragement.* Why had she thought she could be an actress? Right now, she was most definitely vomit-level nervous. And wouldn't that make a great internet meme?

She stepped further into the room and fought the urge to blink against the fluorescent lights that shone down on her. The room was smaller than the one she'd just left and a rectangular table was the only furnishing. It held a round tray, piled high with empty plastic bowls.

A man with stringy hair and glasses that had slid to the end of his nose stared at her with disinterest from where he sat on a padded chair against one wall. A plump middle-aged woman with eyebrows that seemed raised in permanent surprise sat beside him, and a tall man with a scar through one eyebrow leaned against the wall.

Yup. She definitely felt like puking.

"Name?" Glasses asked. He didn't bother introducing himself, but she figured he was the casting director.

"Tamera Hadley. I'm auditioning for the part of waitress." She was proud of how steady her voice sounded.

Glasses grunted and motioned vaguely to the table, like he'd already lost interest. "Ames will read the part of Daniel opposite you. Whenever you're ready."

Ames pushed off the wall, everything from his relaxed posture to his unfocused eyes screaming boredom. He'd probably been reading these same five lines for the past five hours. Tamera didn't recognize him, which meant he was probably not the actor cast in the lead role. Her agent had explained that leads didn't waste their time reading lines with unknown hopefuls auditioning for inconsequential parts.

Ames didn't even bother making eye contact as he slunk to his mark. But that was fine. She would blow them all away with her performance—force them to wake up and take notice of her.

A familiar steely determination washed over Tamera. Her muscles relaxed and head cleared, just like before a Head Honcho competition. She took one deep, steadying breath, allowing time to slow down. Then she picked up the tray and got to work.

The ache of Caleb and Katie's betrayal and the stress of the last month disappeared as Tamera stepped into the role of waitress and became someone else. By her second line, Ames' body language had gone from bored to alert. His movements were purposeful now, his eyes intense and each line delivered with precision. She felt the chemistry change in the room as Glasses and Eyebrows perked up, their hands still on their clipboards as they paid attention to her performance.

A heady sense of freedom eclipsed all her fears, and Tamera gave herself over to the role. This overpowering liberation was why she loved acting so much. It was what had made playing *Eye in the Sky* so intoxicating.

When Tamera finished, she set her tray on the table with a flourish and turned for her critique.

"Well then." Glasses shuffled through a stack of papers, obviously searching for her file. "What did you say your name is?"

She struggled to keep a smile from overtaking her face. Now he was interested. "Tamera Hadley."

"Here you are." He flipped open the folder and peered at it. "You were a contestant on *Eye in the Sky*?"

Don't be ashamed of your work experience. That was the first thing her agent had coached her on. Yes, she'd never had a part in more than a high school play. But four months of being on camera twenty-four hours a day was more experience than most actresses had in years.

"That's correct," Tamera said. "I spent ninety-one days in the house and made it to the final four."

"Very impressive. What other experience do you have with acting?"

She cleared her throat, fighting to keep her tone unapologetic. "I played Abigail in *The Crucible* my senior year."

His eyes flicked back to the file, flipping through the pages. "Yes, I see that here. What about film?"

His disinterest was showing again. Tamera tried not to panic. "I've been on five national talk shows in the past month, discussing my time on *Eye in the Sky*."

"But no movies." She knew it wasn't a question, and he let out a *hmmm.*

"She's represented by Hershel Clark," the woman said, speaking for the first time. Tamera felt her heart leap, and sent the woman a grateful look.

"Yeah, it's in her file," Glasses said, not seeming impressed.

"I've got a very dedicated following on social media that would be an asset when the film releases." Tamera's palms grew damp, but she pressed forward. She hadn't come this far to give up at the first sign of resistance. "I'm also a hard worker and a fast learner. I take direction very well, and am committed to improving my craft. It would be an honor to work on a project as prestigious as this one."

"You and every other up-and-comer in L.A." Glasses set her file aside. Did that mean she'd already been taken out of the running? Or was that pile reserved for actresses who might get a callback? Would they even do callbacks for such a small part? "We'll be in touch with your agent no later than Friday with our decision."

She recognized a dismissal when she saw one. Tamera knew better than to press her luck again—she was gutsy, not stupid. So she stood tall, refusing to let her shoulders slump and show her disappointment. "Thank you for your time."

He waved a hand in a weak acknowledgment but didn't bother to reply. Tamera picked up her purse and exited the way she'd entered, avoiding the eyes of the catty girls still waiting for their chance to prove themselves.

I think it's a no, she texted Drew.

I'm sure you did great.

She yanked open her car door and slid inside, frustration burning through her. How was she supposed to gain experience if no one would hire her without it? That wasn't at all how she'd imagined her first audition going.

"Did you think they'd fall at your feet in awe?" she muttered angrily as she started the car.

The pathetic thing was that part of her had believed the casting director would be impressed by her time on *Eye in the Sky*. Stupid. Clearly jump-starting her acting career was going to take a lot more than one audition.

A call lit up her phone—her real estate partner. She let her car idle in park and answered, trying to sound upbeat. "Hey, Landon."

"Hey." His voice was tight with worry, which had pretty much been the status quo ever since his wife became pregnant.

"What's up?"

"It's Julie. She's struggling to keep anything down again, and the doctors want me to bring her in for fluids."

Poor Julie. Her morning sickness had been awful, and it kept causing one complication after another. "Oh no. I thought she was doing better with the new medication."

"Me too, but I guess it was a fluke. Anyway, I need to ask you a favor."

She ran a hand over her steering wheel, already mentally rearranging her week to fit in whatever clients he needed help with. "Of course. Whatever you need."

"I'm supposed to meet a new client at the office in like an hour. We've got three showings lined up for this afternoon. Can you take him?"

That actually wouldn't require any rearranging at all. Tamera had kept her afternoon open, not sure how long the audition would go. "No problem. Text me the info and I'll take care of everything."

"You're a life saver. I'm sending it now."

Her phone beeped with the addresses. Tamera raised an eyebrow. "This is a higher-end area."

"This guy's got more cash to throw around than our usual clients."

"What's his name?"

The line went silent. Had the call been disconnected? Tamera glanced at the screen. Nope, still ongoing. "Landon?"

"I can't tell you who he is or I'm on the hook for half a million dollars. When you get to the office, let Samantha know you need to sign a nondisclosure."

Whoa. Only public figures cared about nondisclosures. She'd certainly never had to sign one before working with a client, although sometime the senior agents did. Tamera looked at the addresses again, trying to picture the area. The homes in that neighborhood were certainly high-end, but nothing like the mega-mansions hidden in the Los Angeles hills.

"I'll let him know you're coming," Landon said, interrupting Tamera's speculations. "He wanted to ride with me to the showings since he's still not familiar with California traffic."

"Not a problem." Tamera glanced at the fast food bag on her passenger floor. She'd have to remember to throw that in the trash. At least the rest of her sporty red convertible was clean.

"Thanks again. You have no idea how much you're helping me."

"You helped me out for months and I'm happy to return the favor. Tell Julie to take care of herself."

"I will," Landon promised.

They said their goodbyes and hung up. The A/C was finally starting to do its job, cooling the car to a more comfortable temperature. Tamera glanced at her watch, then dropped her phone into the cup holder and put the car in gear. If traffic cooperated, she'd get to the office in enough time to sign the NDA and go over the specs on at least one of the properties before Mr. Nondisclosure arrived.

She really hoped he was the kind of guy who showed up on time for appointments. Curiosity was eating her alive.

Chapter Six

Wyatt crawled down the Los Angeles freeway, feeling more alive than he had in months. His truck had arrived from Texas yesterday, a fully loaded silver Ford F-150 that he'd bought with his first paycheck after being drafted. He gripped the steering wheel in one hand as the warm spring breeze played with his hair and the radio belted out a country hit.

This felt good. Right. For the first time since agreeing to the trade, living in California didn't seem like a punishment. Hopefully he could quickly find a house and get even more settled in his new life. Next week was his first practice with the team, and he was actually looking forward to it.

An automated voice interrupted the song on the radio. "Call from Landon McMillan." Ryder Communications had rolled out Talia On the Move a few months ago, and Wyatt had immediately wondered how he ever lived without it.

"Answer," Wyatt said. There was a pause, then a click as the call was picked up. "Hey, Landon. I'm stuck in traffic, but I'm on my way."

"I'm not," Landon said, and Wyatt heard the weariness in his voice. "I'm really sorry about this, Wyatt, but I'm at the hospital with my wife."

Wyatt's hand tightened on the steering wheel. He didn't know Landon well—had hired him based on a recommendation from an old college teammate—but that couldn't be good. "I'm sorry to hear that. I hope it's nothing serious."

"Me too. She's pregnant and has had a lot of complications."

Wyatt looked at the long line of traffic in front of him and stifled a sigh. The freeway exit was only a mile away, but it'd take him at least ten minutes to inch that far. "That's not good. Don't worry about me—we can reschedule for another time."

"My partner can actually show you the homes today. I didn't tell her your name, but she's very competent and more than willing to sign a nondisclosure. I know how much you value your privacy."

Another real estate agent? Wyatt gnawed on his lip and silently debated whether to take a chance on this unexpected variable. His old teammate had promised that Landon knew how to be both professional and discreet. This new agent was an unknown Wyatt wasn't sure he wanted to deal with.

He could decline the new agent's help and ask Landon to reschedule today's showings for when he was available. Some of the properties might go under contract in the meantime, but more would come on the market. However, a pregnancy sounded like a long-term issue that might mean months before Landon could be of any real help. And no way Wyatt was living in a hotel for that long. He'd only been at the newer economy hotel for three days, but it was getting old fast.

Bobby would be more than happy to recommend a new real estate agent. But even that would take a few days, and Wyatt really wanted to see today's properties.

"I wouldn't hand you over to my partner if I didn't trust her," Landon said, as though sensing Wyatt's hesitation. "She'll take good care of you."

Wyatt nodded, his decision made. "Okay. Thank you."

"No—thank you." Landon's voice filled with relief. "Again, I am so sorry about this."

"It couldn't be helped."

"We'll talk again in a few days."

They said their goodbyes and Wyatt hung up. He trusted Landon's judgment, but still wanted a nondisclosure signed by the new agent before he arrived. "Talia, pull up the nondisclosure document emailed to Landon McMillan."

"Of course, Wyatt." The car was silent for a moment, then Talia said, "I have located the document. How should I proceed?"

"Attach it to an email. Recipient should be Parker-Lane Realty and the subject line should be nondisclosure agreement." Wyatt tapped the steering wheel, realizing he didn't know the name of Landon's partner.

"What would you like the body of the email to say?" Talia asked.

Hmmm. Maybe he should call Landon back and ask for his partner's name and email. It would be safer than sending the email to the agency's main address. But Landon was busy taking care of his wife and unborn child, and Wyatt didn't want to bother him. "The email should say, To Whom It May Concern, Landon McMillan has asked his partner to take over for him today. Please print off this nondisclosure and have her sign it before my arrival in twenty minutes."

"Okay, Wyatt." There was a moment of silence, and then Talia said, "The email is ready to be sent."

"Send it," Wyatt said.

Despite being after six o'clock, the lot at Park-Lane Realty was still half-full of everything from gleaming BMWs to rusted Toyotas. Good. His truck would blend in just fine. Wyatt grabbed a worn baseball cap off the passenger seat and tugged it on, making sure the brim was pulled low over his face. Then he jumped out of the truck and hurried across the parking lot, keeping his head down. Over the last few days, he'd ignored the publicity about his trade as much as possible, but knew from Bobby that the announcement had created quite a buzz.

A blast of cool air filtered over Wyatt as he entered the office. A middle-aged woman with graying hair and sagging arms sat behind a reception desk. A name placard sat on top, and next to her computer monitor he caught a glimpse of a gold picture frame holding a photo of three teenage children. She looked up from the screen, a customer smile plastered across thin lips.

He knew she'd recognized him when her mouth fell open. So much for the baseball cap.

"Mr. James." She rose quickly and caught her leg on the chair, stumbling. One hand reached out to steady herself on the edge of the desk and her cheeks pinked. "It's such a pleasure to meet you."

Wyatt gave what he hoped was a kind smile and extended his hand. "The pleasure is all mine, Samantha."

She blushed again and handed him a paper. "I received your email and had Tamera sign the nondisclosure as soon as she walked in. I'll let her know you're here."

"I appreciate that." Wyatt glanced down at the loopy signature, listening with half an ear as Samantha called Tamera's office.

So this agent's name was Tamera. He squinted, trying to make out the last name on the signature line. Was that an H? Yes, Hadley. Tamera Hadley.

Wait. He read the name again—definitely Tamera Hadley.

The name blinked in his brain louder than a tied score on a JumboTron. Could his new real estate agent really be the adorable brunette from the gym, with the sad eyes and hair clips falling everywhere? After binge watching her entire season of *Eye in the Sky*—and, okay, reading way too many online articles in celebrity gossip magazines—there was no doubt the name at least was the same.

An insane idea flickered through his mind. Was this a ploy by Drew to dig the knife in Wyatt's back just a little deeper? Maybe he'd sent Tamera to that hotel. Somehow maneuvered her into position as his real estate agent. All so ... what? She could tell the paparazzi where Wyatt lived?

No way. This whole thing was just a coincidence. A crazy, insane, unexpectedly exciting coincidence.

The click of heels had his blood pumping through his veins like he'd just run a marathon. No doubt about it—this Tamera Hadley was one and the same. She'd gotten her hair cut since the show finale and now her sleek cappuccino-colored locks just brushed her collarbone. He hadn't noticed its length at the gym since it had been pinned up. Makeup brought attention to her wide and inviting eyes and he fought the urge to run his knuckles along those high cheekbones. A fitted blouse hugged her curves. Dark denim jeans and high heels elongated her legs until he had a hard time looking away.

The camera hadn't done her justice. She'd been beautiful on *Eye in the Sky*. Vulnerable at the gym. But here, in the lobby of Parker-Lane Realty, she was stunning.

Her steps faltered when she recognized him, and then a smile lit up her eyes—and made his knees a little weak. "No way. You're Landon's client?"

He lifted a shoulder in a careless shrug. "Guilty as charged."

She laughed, taking a thin folder from Samantha. "What are the odds?"

"It's quite the coincidence."

Tamera took a step forward and there was something in her expression that made his blood run hot. "I don't believe in coincidences."

Wyatt cleared his throat and took a step back. If the show was to be believed, she was very good friends—maybe even more than friends—with Drew. In a lot of ways, she was everything Wyatt had run away from in San Antonio. He needed to remember that.

"Landon said you preferred me to drive," Tamera said.

"If you don't mind. I'm still not used to the traffic."

Tamera laughed and every hair on Wyatt's body stood at attention. She'd done that on the show—drawn people to her, like moths to a flame, only to snuff out their *Eye in the Sky* life when given the chance. There was a word for women like Tamera. Siren.

He wasn't about to let himself be one of her victims.

Tamera tapped the folder on the desk. "Thanks for printing off the property sheets for me, Sam."

"No problem," Samantha said cheerfully. "It was so nice to meet you, Mr. James."

"You too," Wyatt said.

He followed Tamera to the parking lot, desperately trying not to stare at the view. He fumbled with the nondisclosure agreement, finally managing to fold it into quarters and shove it in his back pocket.

Tamera pressed the unlock button on her keyless remote, and a red Mazda convertible flashed its lights a few rows away. Great. He'd barely fit in that thing, with his long legs and bulky frame.

"Here we are." Tamera frowned at Wyatt. "Sorry, it's kind of small. Are you going to be okay?"

They could take his truck, but he really didn't want to battle traffic. "I'll be fine." He immediately banged a knee on the dashboard, contradicting his claims.

Tamera laughed and pushed a button, causing the top to fold back. "That'll give us a little more room."

"Thanks."

"Gotta keep my clients happy." She winked and slid on her sunglasses.

Wyatt swallowed hard. The curve of her neck was way too appealing from this angle.

"The first property is about thirty minutes away, but then all three homes are really close together."

"Sounds great." Wyatt subtly adjusted, trying to straighten out his legs. A cramp was already forming in one.

"Why don't you tell me what you're looking for in a property?"

He swallowed, forcing himself not to stare as the breeze tousled her hair. "The most important things to me are security and privacy, so a gated community is a must. It needs to have at least four bedrooms and three bathrooms." That way he could have a home office for screenwriting and still have room for when family visited. He and Natalie had grown especially close over the last few years, and she'd promised to visit as often as school allowed. That was one benefit of moving to Los Angeles—Phoenix was now only a short plane ride away. "I also need space for a home gym. And it needs an amazing media room, or space that I convert into one." Geez, when he said it out loud, it didn't sound as frugal as he'd imagined being.

"That's a pretty reasonable wish list. I thought all you celebrities wanted drinking fountains that spit out champagne or whatever."

Wyatt laughed, feeling himself relax. Tamera crawled down the freeway, one hand resting casually on the steering wheel. The sunlight had turned her skin a glowing bronze. "Champagne fountain. That's one I haven't heard."

"Really? It's in Drew's house."

Wyatt barely held back a snort. Drew would have something that ridiculous in his house. What did Tamera see in the guy? He was vain and shallow, and he'd done little to help her on *Eye in the Sky* other than providing a vote. "Not really my thing."

"What is your thing?"

Definitely not beautiful women who spelled trouble. "I'm kind of a movie buff."

"That's so cool." Tamera slammed on her breaks, then darted in between two cars. Wyatt clutched the door handle. He would never get used to California drivers. "Me too."

Wyatt had heard that before. Women always seemed to miraculously like exactly what he did. Becky had been a chameleon, changing her likes and opinions to blend in with his. He hadn't noticed it until the initial pain of the breakup was past. "What kind of stuff are you into?"

"Anything and everything."

Big surprise.

"I want to be an actress. I know it's totally cliché, but I've dreamed about red carpets and Hollywood premiers for as long as I can remember."

Wyatt straightened in his seat. "Really?"

Her cheeks pinked. "Yeah. I actually had an audition today. Just a minor part, but it'd be a great stepping stone."

"Huh. That's actually pretty cool."

"It's something that I love." She ran a hand through her windblown hair, and Wyatt swallowed hard. "I kind of go through phases on movies and TV shows. I'm really into police procedurals right now, but before I went on *Eye in the Sky* I was on an old Hollywood kick. What kinds of movies do you like?"

Her answer felt honest and that surprised Wyatt. "I'm kind of the same as you—it depends on the day. I've been studying action films a lot lately."

"What do you mean, studying?"

Wyatt pulled his baseball cap low over his eyes, suddenly feeling embarrassed. "Uh, I write scripts."

"What?" Tamera jerked the wheel and Wyatt put out a hand so he wouldn't hit the dashboard. "That's amazing. I never would've guessed."

Wyatt shrugged self-consciously. He'd never told anyone but Natalie about his scripts. Why had he suddenly blurted it out to Tamera? "They're probably not any good, but I have fun writing them."

"They're not any good." She waved a hand through the air. "Whatever. You're Wyatt freakin' James. People will throw their money at the box office to see something you wrote."

"It's not like I'll ever sell anything."

"Never say never." Tamera cut across three lanes of traffic and barely made the exit. This woman's driving should be registered as a lethal weapon. "Wow. I guess we have more in common than I realized."

"Yeah, I guess so," Wyatt said. And for some reason, that terrified him.

Chapter Seven

T amera pulled up to the gleaming black iron gate surrounding the community and entered in the passcode, curiosity eating her alive. Manicured trees shaded the driveway, which showed a few cracks —nothing major, but she could see weeds trying to peek through. A stone sign introducing the community sat among dozens of blooming flowers. Ivy climbed up the stone fence surrounding the area.

This community was definitely nice. High end, even. But it was lawyer nice. Doctor nice. Financial planner nice. Not professional athlete nice. Drew wouldn't be caught dead living somewhere like this.

The gate to the community slid open with a low screech, as though the runners needed to be greased. Tamera drove down the tree-lined driveway, trying to ignore the very distracting man sitting beside her. The wind had been playing with his T-shirt the entire trip and driving her mad in the process.

"What do you think of the neighborhood?" Tamera asked as they turned down a street.

"It's nice," Wyatt said noncommittally.

Hmmm. Did that mean he hadn't formed an opinion, or he wasn't impressed?

And why had Drew told her to be careful around Wyatt? She and

Wyatt had talked about their favorite movies the entire thirty-minute drive. They shared a lot of the same tastes, and she'd loved dissecting the plots of some of her favorites with him. But Drew's warning wouldn't leave the back of her mind.

Tamera pulled up the the curb. "Here we are."

The property sat in the middle of the block—not quite as desirable as a corner lot, but the street was quiet and the homes weren't situated too closely together. The terra cotta roof and arched windows had a bit of a Spanish flair, and that wasn't the only thing she immediately disliked about the property. Cracked white stucco was discolored on the west side from sunlight. The driveway needed to be resurfaced and the windows could use a good power wash. It was the kind of house she usually showed to a dentist with four kids.

Tamera cut the engine and tried not to stare as Wyatt unfolded himself from the passenger seat. His shoulders were broad enough to block her view of the house, and what a view it was. Wyatt tipped his ball cap back on his head, then rested his hands on his trim hips. She could see his biceps bulging through the thin cotton of his gray T-shirt.

"It's big," Wyatt said.

Tamera blinked, ripping her gaze from his arms. "Is that a problem?"

He shrugged, and his entire body seemed to move with the roll of his shoulders while her heart sped up to double time. "I'm not sure I need this much space."

"It's a house that can grow with you," Tamera said. "But if you're really not sure about the space, we can look at properties with smaller square footage next time."

"I guess it would be nice when my family visits."

"Absolutely." She headed up the walk. "Do you have a big family?"

"No, it's just my parents and little sister. But we're close."

"That's really cool." Tamera bent down and fiddled with the lock box. "What about you?"

A bitter laugh escaped. "I just have one sister and parents, too. Katie and I don't get along for obvious reasons."

"I can imagine."

Tamera swung open the door, grateful for the distraction. "Here we are."

The house showed its age, with several of the entryway tiles cracked from settling. The air smelled of fresh paint, but she could see from here that the carpet leading up the stairs was matted from use. If she'd been showing this home to her usual clients, she would've gushed over it—the perfect home for a family that could quickly increase in value with a little sweat equity. But for Wyatt?

She turned around, eager to see his reaction, and came face to face with his chest. Tamera took a quick step back, her heart stuttering.

"What do you think?" she breathed.

"It's okay," Wyatt said noncommittally, his eyes not letting go of hers.

She blinked and stepped even further away, trying to clear her head. Going all weak-kneed over Wyatt James was pointless. He could be the most attractive man on the planet—and he just might be—and it wouldn't matter. The only relationship she was having from here on out was with her career.

"What don't you like about it?"

Wyatt cleared his throat, looking around. "This entryway, for starters. I hate it when they go up the full two stories like this. It's such a waste of space."

Tamera barely refrained from rolling her eyes. It was such a guy reaction to be that practical. "Entryways like this make a house feel more open and inviting. It's good for resale."

"I don't plan on moving again for a very long time."

Well, that was an interesting bit of information. Tamera had been following the story on social media and no one could figure out what had made Wyatt James leave the Vigilantes for the Coyotes. She watched as he stepped into the kitchen and ran a hand over the tile countertops. Did someone live in California that he wanted to be closer to? It was the only thing that made sense.

"The pantry's kind of small," Wyatt said, his head hidden by the doors and his voice muffled.

Right. She was here to sell a house, not ogle Wyatt.

"There's quite a bit of cabinet space," Tamera said. "Hopefully that would help compensate."

He nodded, shutting the door. "The team nutritionist makes pretty much all my meals, but Natalie likes to cook so I try and keep things stocked for when she visits."

"Natalie?"

"My little sister. She's a junior at Arizona State."

Relief flowed through Tamera, taking her by surprise. For a second, she'd thought Natalie was his new girlfriend. He'd broken up with a Vigilantes cheerleader a few months back—barely a blip on the celebrity gossip radar—but she couldn't imagine someone like Wyatt would stay single long. He was down-to-earth and easy to talk to. Girls would be crazy not to snatch him up.

Other girls. Not her, obviously.

"Does she visit often?" Tamera asked.

"Mostly during school breaks." Wyatt shrugged. "I got her and my parents season tickets. Now that my dad's retired, he and my mom plan on coming up from Arizona pretty often."

"Thus your need for more bedrooms."

Wyatt nodded and moved past her into the dining room. Sliding glass doors let in lots of natural light and a dated chandelier hung low over the table for twelve. "It'll be nice to see them more often, now that I'm closer to home again."

Tamera leaned against the door frame, trying to keep her tone casual. "Is that why you transfered to the Coyotes?"

"Not exactly." Wyatt motioned to the room. "I like more open floor plans, I think. I'm not much for formal dining rooms."

"Noted." Tamera followed him into the living room, which boasted twelve-foot vaulted ceilings. "So what was the reason you were traded?"

Wyatt glanced over at her but said nothing.

"Come on. You have to know speculations are going wild. The Vigilantes are the team to beat this year. And the Coyotes are ... well, not."

"McKinley's got big plans for the team, and the new recruits seem promising."

A canned response if she'd ever heard one. "Maybe, with a few years of hard training, the Coyotes can be back in it. But this year?" She shrugged. "You have to see the writing on the wall."

Wyatt adjusted his hat, not meeting her eyes. "I guess I was ready for a change. Things were a little tense in Texas."

"I heard about the breakup."

"Really?"

Tamera shrugged. "It was a small article in one magazine. I keep up on those kinds of things. Aspiring actress, remember? Got to keep dialed in on Hollywood gossip."

Wyatt grunted. "It was never going to work out with Becky."

"I know what it's like to go through an awkward breakup on television. I'm sorry you had to go through something similar." Becky had apparently been caught with another man—the article never did say who—and that was that.

Wyatt's face softened and he shook his head. "No, I'm the one who's sorry. I can't imagine having all my dirty laundry aired like yours was. You handled it so well on the show. Very classy. I admire how you never talked badly about Katie or Caleb."

Tamera folded her arms, a slow grin spreading across her face. "You watched *Eye in the Sky*."

Wyatt's ears turned red and he ran a hand over his buzzed hair. "I was curious after meeting you."

"Well, color me surprised, Wyatt James. I thought I made a total idiot of myself."

He laughed, heading up the stairs to the second floor of the house. "I was so surprised to find someone in the gym."

"That makes two of us. I had no idea I wasn't alone." She sobered, remembering the way her chest had physically hurt that night with the pain of Katie and Caleb's betrayal.

They'd posted photos that morning of the two of them riding horses on the beach. It had taken a lot of effort not to react with an angry emoji.

Wyatt opened a door at the top of the stairs, revealing a small laundry room with barely enough room to open the appliance doors. "Seems like you and Drew got to be pretty good friends while on the show."

"Yeah." Tamera licked her lips, not sure if she should continue. Maybe mention it, but keep it playful? "Drew told me to stay away from you. But you don't seem like trouble to me."

Wyatt grunted. "Drew and I aren't exactly best friends."

"What happened between you two?"

"Oh, you know. Guy stuff." He pointed to a doorway at the end of the hallway. "I'm guessing that's the master bedroom?"

"Yeah, probably." Tamera took the hint and let the subject drop as she followed him into the master bedroom, but that didn't stop her mind from going nuts with the possibilities.

Maybe Drew and Wyatt just had conflicting personalities. No use speculating. Clearly, neither man was going to tell her what had really happened. At the end of the day, what did it matter? After Wyatt closed on a house, they'd never have to see each other again.

"The show certainly tried to convince everyone something was going on between you and Drew," Wyatt said.

No way was she letting Wyatt operate under that assumption. And no, she most definitely didn't want to more closely examine why it made her cheeks flush with rage to think of Wyatt assuming there was something between her and Drew. "If I had a dollar for every time someone asked about our supposed showmance, I wouldn't have to sell you a house."

"I'll take that as a 'no,' then."

"Drew's only interested in what he can't have." Tamera peered into the master bathroom. Two steps led up to a giant soaker tub and a spacious shower sat beside it. "We are most definitely just friends."

"Good friends?"

"Good friends with zero benefits. You're really not going to tell me what the deal is between you two?"

"Just different approaches to life, I guess." Wyatt pointed to the tub. "I know guys aren't supposed to take baths, but a tub like that would be awesome. Sometimes it's really nice to soak after a hard practice. Helps relax the muscles."

And now she had the image of Wyatt submerged in bubbles, his broad shoulders not quite below the surface of the water. "Okay. I'm adding 'soaker tub' to your wish list."

Now if she could just stop mentally adding Wyatt James to hers.

They headed back downstairs to admire the backyard. Sunlight reflected off the clear blue water of the pool and an impressive outdoor kitchen ran along the backside of the home.

"You've got a way with the camera," Wyatt said as he stared across the yard. "I can see why you were so popular with viewers. You'll do great as an actress."

The audition came rushing back and Tamera sighed. "Maybe, if I ever get a part."

"You'll make it," Wyatt said, his tone confident.

"Of course you think that, Mr. One-in-a-Million. How many little boys actually grow up to be pro football players?"

He laughed and the sound sent shivers down her spine. "Okay, I see your point. But seriously, you were great. I could never be that natural in front of the camera."

He was a little stiff in interviews, but she wasn't going to say it.

"The team's asked me to shoot a few promo spots for the season and I'm already dreading it. Every time that camera turns on, I clam up."

"You do fine on the field," Tamera said.

"That's because my head's in the game and I'm not thinking about it."

Tamera hoped they had Wyatt shirtless in the commercial. It'd sell tickets for sure. "See? You just have to shut off your brain and become someone else for a moment."

"Yeah, so simple."

"I'm sure you'll do great."

"If not, maybe they'll fire me and convince one of the other guys to do it." Wyatt smirked. "Maybe I should purposefully do really bad."

"I don't think you're that kind of guy."

"Yeah, I guess not." He let out a sigh. "I do love the landscaping on this house, but I can't imagine myself living here. It just doesn't have the right feel, you know?"

Tamera nodded. For a moment, she'd almost forgotten they were here to look at a house. "I totally understand. Let's go see what the next house holds."

Chapter Eight

W yatt drove carefully toward the Coyotes stadium as his sister's chatter filled the cab of his truck, distracting him from worry over his first day with the team.

"I think it might be another week or two before I can come out and visit you," Natalie said. "Mom and Dad mentioned coming out there in June and I might just wait until then. This semester is burying me in homework."

"You guys should probably wait until I have a house anyway." Wyatt slammed on his breaks as traffic suddenly halted.

"Get one with a pool, okay? I've been dying for a swim."

Wyatt laughed. "I'll see what I can do."

"I never did ask you if you found anything promising the other day. I guess if you had, I would've heard about it."

"Nothing worth putting an offer on," Wyatt agreed. Although the time spent with Tamera definitely hadn't been a waste.

"Hopefully something comes up ASAP. The sooner you can settle in and hunker down, the better. People are super suspicious about your trade."

Tamera had said the same thing. Wyatt gripped the steering wheel. If Drew didn't keep his mouth shut...

But he had no reason to go public now. It would raise too many questions, since the injury had been five months ago.

"The whole thing is just so stupid," Natalie continued. "Becky is a snake and so is Drew."

Wyatt wasn't about to argue with her.

"How are classes going?" Wyatt asked, ready for a subject change.

Natalie prattled on about a professor she hated and one she had a crush on while Wyatt listened with half an ear. He turned into the stadium parking lot, nerves making his throat tighten.

His first day. He gripped the steering wheel tighter. Being the new kid on the block was never fun.

"Are you listening?" Natalie asked.

"Sorry. I guess I'm a little distracted."

"Nervous about your first day?" she guessed.

"I'm sure everything will be fine. Can I call you back later?"

A dramatic sigh filled the line. "Oh, I suppose. Scope out the hot guys for me, okay?"

"Uh, we don't *scope each other out*. Especially not in the locker room."

He could practically see her eyes rolling through the phone line. "Whatever. I demand you introduce me to everyone when I come visit."

"Let me meet them first, okay?"

"Just this once. Good luck!"

"Thanks." He was going to need it.

Wyatt got out of his truck and stared up at the ancient stadium looming above him. Scaffolding lined one entire side and painters were changing the exterior from a scuffed brown to a dark gray. Looked like Luke was wasting no time updating the stadium. Maybe the Coyotes really would turn around under his ownership.

Two other players met each other on the opposite side of the parking lot and slapped hands. They ambled inside, their deep voices carrying on the still morning air. Wyatt took a deep breath and hiked his duffel bag higher on his shoulder. He needed to go outside his comfort zone today and make friends so the others didn't see him as an outsider. At least he wouldn't be the only new face, although he was the only trade—the others were all new picks from the draft.

The concrete breezeways of the stadium echoed each of Wyatt's steps. Laughter floated from the direction of the locker room, but Wyatt was alone in the hallway except for a few painters who were stenciling the team logo on one wall.

A door opened along the wall and Luke stepped out. He grinned when he saw Wyatt and held out a hand for a shake.

"Ready for your first day?" Luke asked.

"Ready as I'll ever be."

"The guys are great. You'll fit right in." He walked backward down the hallway. "They're doing the first shoot for the commercial after practice, right?"

Yeah, because meeting the team and having his first practice with the Coyotes wasn't enough stress for one day. "Yup."

"Can't wait to see the footage. It's going to be great." Luke waved and then disappeared around a corner.

Wyatt shook his head and pushed open the door to the locker room. He just had to take today one step at a time. Right now, all he had to do was find his locker and say hello to whoever was nearby.

The Coyotes locker room had a low ceiling and peeling paint, with narrow lockers crammed next to each other—a definite step down from the sleek lines and open space he'd enjoyed with the Vigilantes. Men stood around the room in various states of dress, laughing and talking as they discussed what they'd done while on break.

Wyatt made his way around the periphery of the room until he found the locker where his new jersey hung proudly, the name *James* prominently displayed on the back alongside his number. The gold and blue looked out of place after three seasons of black and green.

You're making the best of the situation, he reminded himself. He had his truck, his writing, and soon he'd have a new house. Things weren't all bad.

A man dropped his duffel bag in the locker next to Wyatt's. He was tall and muscular, with dark skin and a shaved head. Tattoos covered both arms. "You must be James."

"That's me," Wyatt said.

"I'm Tyrone Miller." He held out a hand and pulled Wyatt in for quick back clap. "Good to meet you."

"You too." The band squeezing Wyatt's chest relaxed ever so slightly. He'd had his first introduction, which was always the hardest part of a new team.

"You're gonna like California," Tyrone said with confidence. "Don't you be thinking 'bout those Vigilantes for a minute. They may have more wins, but we got McKinley now and everything's gonna change."

"I'm looking forward to it."

A tall man with sun-bronzed skin, shaggy blond hair, and tightly coiled muscles paused just inside the locker room and held up his hands. "Schroeder in the house!" he yelled, then let out a hoot.

Half a dozen men hooted in response, and then started whipping each other with their shirts. Schroeder slapped their butts and made his way to the other side of the room.

Cortney Schroeder was one of the few exceptional players on the Coyotes and it looked like he knew it. Why were quarterbacks always so blasted arrogant? They acted like the sun rose and set on their command.

Tyrone rolled his eyes and pulled cleats out of his duffel bag. "Let me give you a piece of advice, James."

"Okay," Wyatt said easily.

"Whatever you do, don't get on Schroeder's bad side. He'll make your life miserable in practice."

Wyatt gave a sharp nod, grinding his teeth together in frustration. He'd hoped to escape the Drews of the world in California, but it seemed he'd asked the universe for too much.

"Let me introduce you around," Tyrone said. "We've got some good guys on the team."

"Thanks." Wyatt offered Tyrone a genuine smile. His locker mate's friendliness went a long way to easing Wyatt's anxieties.

As Tyrone made introductions, Wyatt felt himself loosening up. The other guys welcomed him with friendly smiles and seemed genuinely happy to have him on the team. But then Tyrone paused in front of Schroeder's locker.

When Tyrone spoke, his tone was flat. "This is Schroeder."

"Wyatt James, in the flesh. Never thought I'd be on a team with you." Schroeder held out a fist and Wyatt reluctantly nudged it with his own. "Team party at my house this weekend. If you don't show up, I'll take it as a personal insult."

"Sounds great," Wyatt said with feigned enthusiasm. "Send me the deets and I'll be there."

"Awesome. Any lady friends are more than welcome to accompany you." Schroeder backed away and pointed his fingers at Wyatt. "Saturday."

"Saturday," Wyatt agreed, the word souring in his mouth.

"If you don't show up, he really will make your life miserable," Tyrone muttered as they walked out of the locker room. "I'll pick you up at the hotel and we can drive over together. His house is kind of hard to find in the dark."

"Thanks," Wyatt said. At least he'd made one friend today.

Conditioning with the team went well, and by the end of the practice, Wyatt felt as though he'd begun tentative friendships with a few of the guys, Tyrone included. Back in the locker room, he took his time showering. He didn't want the other guys, especially the veterans of the team, to know he'd been chosen as the face of the upcoming marketing campaign. Telling them he was headed back to the field for his first shoot felt like an awkward way to end his first day.

The room was nearly empty when Wyatt made his way back to his locker, but Tyrone was still packing his bag.

"You leaving, James?" Tyrone asked.

"Not yet." Wyatt ran a hand through his hair. "I've got a few things to do first."

Tyrone raised an eyebrow. "Okay."

Wyatt slowly zipped his bag closed. It would probably be more awkward now if he said nothing, because eventually Tyrone would find out. "Mr. Ryder asked me to help with the new marketing campaign. He's running a few commercials and ads to try and up ticket sales. I'm meeting the crew on the field in ten minutes."

Schroeder popped out of the showers, a towel slung around his waist. Wyatt tensed. How had he not realized Schroeder was still here?

"What's that, James?" Schroeder demanded.

Wyatt eyed him warily. "It's nothing."

"Seems like TV spots should be reserved for the quarterback."

"Just doing what I'm told." Wyatt held up his hands. "Trust me, I didn't ask for the screen time."

Schroeder's jaw clenched and his eyes narrowed. But finally he grunted and walked away.

Tyrone clapped Wyatt on the shoulder and shook his head. "Is Mr. Ryder trying to paint a target on your back?"

"No kidding."

Tyrone jerked his thumb toward where Schroeder had just stormed out. "Good luck with that."

"Yeah."

"See you tomorrow." Tyrone saluted and left.

It took a few more minutes for Wyatt to convince himself to head out to the field. It had been totally transformed in the forty minutes since practice ended. Artificial lights were hoisted up on tall poles and cameras on dollies were positioned at various angles around the fifty-yard line.

Wyatt swallowed hard, fighting the urge to run back into the locker room. He could throw a football all day, but talking to a camera felt like a Herculean task.

A woman in a loose-fitting white blouse and trendy red glasses crossed the field. Wyatt winced as her spiky heels dug into the soft grass of the field. She didn't seem to notice or care and latched onto his arm. "Come with me, Mr. James," she said, her tone light and airy. "Hair and makeup is this way, then I'll send you over to wardrobe."

Wyatt reached up, running a hand across his closely cropped locks. What were they going to do, curl it?

The woman laughed, as though sensing the direction of his thoughts. "Don't worry, you'll still feel like yourself when we're done."

Like he'd ever feel comfortable in makeup.

Two hours later, Wyatt most definitely did not feel like himself. He was starting to sweat under the intense heat of the lights and the director was struggling to hide his growing frustration.

"You're too tense, Wyatt." The director rose from his chair and walked across the field. The man was probably in his mid-fifties, with a soul patch and shaved scalp. He rolled his shoulders. "Take a few deep breaths. Try to relax. It's only a few lines."

Relax. Yeah, right. But Wyatt took a deep breath, then nodded. "Okay. Let's try again."

The director took his chair. "Action!"

Wyatt gave a strained smile and began walking down the field, the football clutched in one arm. "Hi." His tone sounded flat even to his own ears. "I'm Wyatt James, the newest offensive lineman for the Los Angeles Coyotes." He finished reciting the memorized script, then paused as he'd been directed for the final frame.

"Cut." The director rubbed his eyes, then sighed. "That's a wrap for today, folks."

Wyatt's shoulders slumped. "I told Mr. Ryder I was no good at this."

The director clapped Wyatt on the shoulder. "You're doing great."

Wyatt snorted.

"You're doing okay," the director amended. "I think we've got enough footage for this piece. We can start working on the next one tomorrow."

Wyatt nodded. The evening had been a complete disaster and he'd totally failed Luke and Coach McKinley. Was there such a thing as an acting tutor? Because he definitely needed one.

Twenty minutes later, he slipped on his jacket and pulled his phone out of his duffel bag to check for messages.

Sent a few new listings to you, Landon texted. **Julie's still in the hospital, but Tamera is happy to take you to any of them. Really sorry to be so flaky.**

Tamera. Just the sight of her name had Wyatt's stomach doing roller coasters.

He tapped his phone against his leg and glanced around at the crew busily dismantling the equipment that had been used to shoot the worst TV commercial in the history of ever. Tamera had been flawless on *Eye in the Sky*. Maybe he should ask her for a few pointers. Seemed like he'd be seeing more of her than he'd planned.

He quickly texted Landon back. **Don't worry about it. I'll let Tamera know if I want to see any of the listings.**

It was probably a good idea to go check out the properties regardless of whether he wanted to make an offer. He needed to get an idea of what was available in his price range and what compromises he might have to make. The fact that Tamera would take him to the showings was beside the point.

Back at the hotel, he perused the five new listing and was pleasantly surprised. Landon had done well—Wyatt was very interested in at least two of them. He quickly texted Tamera before he could talk himself out of it.

Landon said you might be able to take me to a few properties.
Absolutely. :) Which ones did you want to see?

He sent her the listing numbers, along with his availability that week.

I'll let you know when I've got them scheduled, Tamera responded.

Thanks.

Wyatt set his phone down on the small desk in his hotel room and raised his arms above his head. This was about seeing houses—nothing more, nothing less. If it happened to come up, he might ask Tamera for a few pointers on how to make the TV spots go better.

This was strictly professional. He'd make sure to keep it that way.

Chapter Nine

T amera pushed herself to run faster on the treadmill and focused on keeping her breathing even and steady. The condo gym only held two other people and thankfully neither were paying attention to her.

She hadn't gotten the part. Helpless frustration made her ribs ache every time she thought about it. She'd really given her all in that audition, but Hershel said that in the end they'd decided to go with someone more experienced.

Experienced. Ha! If twelve weeks in the *Eye in the Sky* house wasn't experience, then Tamera didn't know what was. She'd put on the performance of her life every day on that show just to stay in the game. And it had worked for ninety-one days.

Her feet thudded rhythmically against the treadmill belt as her thoughts turned to the other stress occupying most of her attention these days—Wyatt. They were meeting tomorrow afternoon to look at houses again. What was it about him that made her lose all rational thought?

Maybe football players were her kryptonite and she'd never realized it until now. She'd gotten drunk on that football date with Luke Ryder and started a fight with the frat boys from the opposing team in the row behind them. That had ended with Luke getting drenched in beer and Tamera being the punchline of late night television jokes for months. Next she'd gotten trapped into a showmance with Drew on *Eye in the Sky*. And okay, maybe that hadn't been an awful decision. He was a good friend, after all. But ultimately her alliance with the formidable Drew had gotten her voted off the show right before the finale. And now she was daydreaming about Wyatt, a guy she'd been warned to stay away from.

Wait. Maybe football wasn't the common denominator. Maybe it was Caleb. All of those things had happened because of him, too. She wouldn't have gotten drunk on her date with Luke if she hadn't just found out about Caleb's engagement to Katie. She wouldn't have gone on *Eye in the Sky* if not for becoming an internet sensation because of the Luke date. And she never would've met Wyatt if she hadn't been in San Antonio for Katie and Caleb's wedding.

Okay, so maybe some of those were a bit of a stretch. Whatever.

Her rubbery legs protested each step and she realized she'd run nearly twelve miles now. At least all this stress had one positive side effect. She hadn't exercised this much in months.

Why wouldn't Drew just tell her what was so awful about Wyatt? It would be so much easier to get him out of her head if she knew why she should. Wyatt's shy grin and easy manner were breaking through her defenses, despite her best efforts to keep them up.

Back in her condo she took a long shower, wishing the painfully hot spray could wash away her conflicting emotions as easily as it washed away her sweat. She grabbed her phone, ready to spend an hour on social media, but froze when she saw the blinking text icon. The contact had been deleted from her phone a long time ago, but she'd recognize that number anywhere.

Why was Caleb texting her while on his honeymoon?

She clicked open the text, trepidation making her heart pound so hard she worried she'd puke. The three words he'd texted sent panic through her entire being.

I miss you.

Her hands shook and she dropped the phone into her lap as her breath came in quick gasps. She tapped her forehead with a finger and muttered, "Think, think, think."

She should ignore the text completely, like he'd ignored her for the past year. He was her brother-in-law, for heaven's sake. She'd been the maid of honor at his wedding. Had that really only been a week ago?

She had to know why he was contacting her now, after everything they'd been through. After so much time.

Why are you texting me? Her fingers shook so badly that it took three tries to get all the words spelled correctly. She glanced at the clock. What time was it in the Bahamas? Where was Katie?

The answer was almost immediate. **I made a mistake.**

Tears blurred Tamera's vision and she blinked quickly to try and force them back. She'd dreamed for months of hearing those words, but now they only made her physically sick. **It's a little late for that.**

I should never have cheated on you with Katie.

She let out a hollow laugh, her fingers flying over the keyboard. **No kidding.**

Things were new and exciting with her.

Translation: things had become boring between them. Tamera blinked, refusing to let the tears fall. She'd liked finally being in a relationship where she was comfortable wearing ratty pajamas and no makeup for a night in.

You shouldn't text me anymore, Tamera said. **You made your choice. Now you've got to live with it.**

We'll be back from our honeymoon next week. I could suggest taking a trip to California to visit you. Katie misses you. I think she'd go for it.

Tamera covered her mouth, fighting back the bile that rose in her throat. How had she dated him for three years and never seen his true colors? **That will NEVER EVER happen. I won't do to Katie what she did to me.**

I think I still love you.

I'm not a cheater. And if I ever did love you—and I'm not sure that I did—you killed that the moment you slept with my sister.

I can't stop thinking about you.

Tamera clenched her phone so hard she worried it might break. She leaned her head against the back of the couch, feeling like the temperature had suddenly dropped twenty degrees. **You're on your honeymoon. With my sister. Do you seriously not see how messed up that is?**

I said I was sorry. What more do you want?

Don't ever text me again. Her hands shook so badly that it took two tries to finally push *send*.

She sat there in her silent condo, trembling as the adrenaline left her body. Not once in her life had she ever fallen for someone who was anything but bad news. She'd thought Toujour was the answer to her horrendous taste in men, but that had ended in disaster, too.

Maybe there was some truth to Drew's claims that Wyatt was bad news. Why else would she be crushing on him?

In the next moment, she was calling Drew. When he picked up, she could hear loud music pulsing in the background. She glanced at the clock. What kind of party would be happening at two in the afternoon? That meant it was only four o'clock in Texas, which was still pretty early.

At the moment, she didn't care. "He's texting me," she blurted before Drew could even say *hello*.

"Whoa." She heard a door close and the music died away. "Slow down. What are you talking about?"

"Caleb." She bit her lip and brushed back the traitorous tear that escaped down her cheek. "They're still on their honeymoon and he's trying to get back together with me. After a year of radio silence. An entire year! Can you believe it? I just..." She growled, unable to put her swirling feelings into words.

"Wait, he's texting you? Did he say that he wants you back?"

"Sort of."

"So he's leaving Katie?"

She laughed, running a shaking hand through her hair. "Oh no. He wants to have his cake and eat it, too."

Drew swore on the other end of the line. "That's messed up."

"You're telling me." She grabbed a blanket off the back of the couch and pulled it around her shoulders. "What's wrong with me, Drew?

Why do I always go for the creeps or the losers or the men who will break my heart?"

"There's nothing wrong with you." He was quiet for a moment and she clutched the phone tighter. "Sometimes guys just have bad judgment. They do things they don't mean to do. Nobody's perfect."

Is that what had happened with Wyatt—a moment of imperfection that resulted in Drew's bad opinion? She was quiet for a moment, then asked, "What did Wyatt do, Drew?"

"Whoa, hold up. How did we get on this subject?"

She snuggled deeper into the blankets, trying not to think about the way Wyatt's brown eyes sucked her in. "He just seemed so nice when I ran into him at the gym."

"Yeah, and we already established you have bad taste in men."

"I'm friends with you," she shot back.

He didn't laugh. "It's not like you'll ever see him again, so what does it matter?"

Tamera fingered a frayed end of the blanket, not sure what she could say. She'd signed an NDA, so she couldn't tell Drew she was selling Wyatt a house. Not unless she had half a million dollars to fork over for breaking the contract.

Drew swore. "You ran into him somewhere, didn't you?"

"There are like four million people in L.A."

"You didn't answer my question."

"I just want to know, okay? What did he do that was so awful?"

Drew's heavy breathing echoed through the line. "Don't do anything you'll regret, Tamera."

Her entire dating history read like a bad report card. "Thanks for the advice, Mom."

"I'm worried about you," he said gruffly. "Do you need me to come out there and screen your dates or something?"

She laughed, pulling the blanket more tightly around her. "Yeah, guys are lining up at my door."

"I don't blame them one bit. Ignore Caleb. He doesn't deserve you."

"Thanks, Drew," Tamera said softly.

"Anytime."

They said their goodbyes and hung up. Caleb hadn't texted her back

—a small miracle. But Wyatt had texted. She hated her heart for giving a leap at the sight of his name.

I've got to stay late at work tomorrow. Don't think I'll have time to backtrack to the real estate office. We can meet at the stadium, or I can meet you at the first property.

She wanted to meet at the stadium. For reasons she didn't want to examine too closely, she was eager to spend more time in the car with Wyatt. Conversation had flowed and she'd felt so safe with him. But it was unprofessional to make that kind of decision. **Whatever you're comfortable with is fine with me.**

A moment later, her phone buzzed with his reply. **Is it okay if we meet at the stadium, or is that too far out of your way?**

She clutched the phone, unable to stop the grin that spread across her face. **No problem at all. See you tomorrow.**

Can't wait.

Chapter Ten

Wyatt trudged out of the empty stadium, feeling like a total failure. This shoot had gone even worse than the last one. He hadn't believed that was possible. At least he'd been on his game during practice. The guys seemed to be warming up to him, Schroeder excluded, and Wyatt was settling into his place on the team.

He made his way toward his truck, eyes scanning the parking lot for Tamera's convertible. A white minivan sat a few spots over from his four-by-four truck, and half a dozen shiny cars and SUVs were a few rows over from that, but otherwise the lot was empty.

These houses better be spectacular. Right now, he really needed something to go right in his life.

A woman stepped out of the white minivan. She wore a sleeveless blouse and flirty knee-length skirt, and her short brown hair blew in the breeze.

He took a hesitant step closer and squinted. Sunglasses obscured half her face, but she raised her hand and waved. Where did Tamera get a minivan? Wyatt picked up the pace and crossed the parking lot in record time.

Tamera slid her sunglasses to the top of her head and motioned to her new wheels. "What do you think?"

He thought Tamera looked way too attractive and he was entering dangerous territory. "I didn't peg you as the minivan type."

She laughed. "It's Landon's. Well, I guess technically it's his wife's. I thought you'd be more comfortable in this than in my convertible."

An odd warmth filled his chest. "You didn't need to do that."

"I know." She flashed him a grin. "Get in. Hopefully your ego doesn't take too big a bruising if anyone recognizes you."

He climbed into the van and stretched his legs. "This is great."

She probably would've done the same for any client. Going out of her way to make sure he was comfortable didn't mean anything other than she was good at her job.

Tamera pulled onto the road, following the GPS's directions. "How was practice?"

He blinked in surprise. It had been a long time since a woman other than his mom or sister had asked him about his day. "Good. We played well today and I feel like I'm getting to know the guys a little better."

"What are they like? It's so hard to tell from watching them on the field. Schroeder seems like such a powerhouse, on and off the field."

Of course she'd be enamored by the team's playboy quarterback. Wyatt swallowed hard and looked away, his foot twitching against the floorboard. "Schroeder's definitely something else."

Tamera rested her arm on the windowsill and pressed her fingers into her hair. "I can't believe I'm helping Wyatt James find a house. Every time I think about it, I realize how nuts it is."

"You're friends with Drew Dempsey. How is knowing me weird?"

She laughed and accelerated onto the freeway. "Drew is Drew. I guess I was a little starstruck the first day, but I got over that pretty quickly once we started playing the game." She flashed him a grin. "I'll let you in on a little secret. I was never much of a Dempsey fan on the field. Sometimes he's lazy in his approach and I don't always agree with his plays. You, though ... well, I've admired you since you were first drafted."

Wyatt could almost feel his head growing two sizes too big under her praise. She was probably just stroking his ego, because he had yet to meet a woman who preferred him over Drew. "You're a big football fan?"

"Pro more than college, but yeah. Sometimes I love football too much. I can be pretty competitive."

Eye in the Sky had certainly shown that to be true. He'd loved watching her give her everything in the Head Honcho competitions, and couldn't help silently cheering every time she won.

"A competitive nature isn't bad," Wyatt said. Attractive, maybe. Okay, definitely.

She snorted. "Yeah. Tell that to Luke Ryder."

"There were extenuating circumstances. I'm pretty sure America's forgiven you after *Eye in the Sky*." Wyatt shifted in his seat as she slowed the van for a turn. This was definitely loads more comfortable than her convertible.

"Yeah, I guess. But those darn internet memes still haunt me. I'm hoping a serious acting career will make everyone forget that nightmare for good."

"Did you hear back from the audition yet?"

She fidgeted, running a hand through her hair. "I didn't get the part. It's fine, though. I've got another audition this weekend. Something's bound to stick eventually, right?"

He thought of his own afternoon spent in front of the cameras and winced. The way he'd gotten progressively worse with each take had surpassed pathetic and almost looped back around to impressive.

"Uh-oh. I know that look. You hated me on *Eye in the Sky*, didn't you? It's okay. I can take the truth."

"No," Wyatt said quickly. "It's not that. You did awesome on the show."

Her grip relaxed on the steering wheel. "Well, that's a relief."

"It was pretty clever how you pitted everyone against each other. It took a long time for everyone to figure out you were really running the house."

"If I'd been just a little more clever, maybe I would've won."

Drew had been the downfall of her game—his big mouth had tipped off some key players and ultimately resulted in Tamera going home. But Wyatt wasn't about to get into that conversation. "I was actually thinking about how bad my own acting is. Mr. Ryder asked me to do some commercials for the team and I think the director's ready to quit."

"I'm sure that's not true."

Wyatt snorted, thinking of the director's tightly clenched jaw. "Pretty sure it is. Every time the camera turns on, I freeze."

"I could give you some pointers. I mean, if you're okay with accepting acting advice from someone who can't seem to land a role."

Red neon warning signs were flashing in his brain. There was a line of attraction between him and Tamera that he should run screaming from. Instead, he said, "That'd be great. Thanks."

It wasn't because he wanted to spend more time with her, he reassured himself. He really did need some acting help, otherwise he'd humiliate himself in the commercial.

Tamera pulled up to a stone-and-stucco home in neutral tones, nestled in the middle of a cul-de-sac. It was set back from the road, with a circular driveway passing by the front door. Wyatt unfolded himself from the car, instantly liking the vibe of this place. The craftsman style gave it a more modern feel than the previous properties they'd seen. Pillars supported the front porch and potted plants hung between them. The landscaping was breathtaking, filled with rich brown soil, colorful flowers, and green grass that begged someone to lay down and watch for shapes in the clouds. He hoped the inside was just as inviting.

"Shall we?" Tamera asked, giving him a smile that had his knees melting.

He nodded. "Looks promising."

Wyatt stepped inside, already loving this property. The entryway managed to be spacious without wasting space and opened into a living room with overstuffed furniture that made the room seem cozy. A staircase led upstairs, and the living room flowed into an open dining room and kitchen.

"I love the open floor plan," Wyatt said.

"It has a nice flow," Tamera agreed.

Wyatt passed through the living room to the kitchen. Tamera's heels clicked against the gray wood flooring, reminding him of her nearness with every step. The cabinets were a cheery white, the countertops some sort of gray solid surface.

"Quartz counters are really popular right now," Tamera said, running her hand along the top of it. "Very nice. And the color scheme is spot-on. They really did their homework when building this place." She pointed to the floor. "They went with the extra wide baseboards and crown molding around the ceiling. It's details like those that push a home over the top in terms of value."

Wyatt opened the pantry and admired the size. More than enough room to stock all the protein drinks he wanted. "These are the kinds of details that make a home valuable to me."

Tamera laughed. "What is it with you and big pantries? Does Natalie really cook that much?"

"I've got lots of protein drinks and energy bars to store, too. But Natalie is a pretty amazing baker. She's always tempting me with brownies and cookies and pies. It's downright evil during the season."

"I think Natalie needs to let me sample some of this stuff."

"I'll tell her you said so." He had a feeling Tamera and Natalie would get along great, and it made his stomach feel like he'd just swallowed a liter of soda.

Down a hallway he found an office with glass French doors. Built-in bookcases lined one wall. Wyatt instantly imagined himself lounging in his cushioned office chair, penning a script about a doe-eyed woman filled with spunk and the professional athlete who was putty in her hands.

Nope. He definitely wasn't going to write that script.

Tamera nudged his side with her shoulder and flames of attraction had his arm hair standing on end. "Think you can negotiate your multi-million dollar trades comfortably in here?"

"No more trades for me."

She raised one eyebrow. "Really?"

He shrugged. "It's not a secret that my career has a shelf life and I'm nearing the end."

"So what are your plans for after retirement? Maybe take that secret script-writing hobby and become a Hollywood bigwig?"

He glanced again at the office. Movie posters of films he'd written would look awesome on the wall. "I guess we'll see."

Her hand brushed his arm, instantly making his mouth go dry. "I can't wait to see what you do next, Wyatt James. Whatever it is, I know it'll be amazing."

This woman was going to drive him slowly, deliciously insane.

Wyatt followed her up the stairs, forcing himself not to stare as she made the climb. He scrambled for something—anything—to get his mind off the ridiculous chemistry zipping between them. Did she feel it?

Tamera flipped on the lights in the bedroom at the top of the stairs. A television hung on one wall, but the decor lacked any personality and screamed guest room.

"Was it hard to leave your job for three months while you did *Eye in the Sky*?" Wyatt asked.

Tamera leaned against the door frame, allowing him the space to examine the room on his own. "Not really. I was very lucky. Most contestants have to quit, but I took a leave of absence and handed my clients over to Landon. The show takes care of food and everything, so there are no living expenses while you're in the house other than whatever bills you're still paying for at home. Once you make it in the top ten you're paid a stipend for each week you remain on the show. It ended up working out pretty well."

"How did you end up auditioning?" He wanted so badly to peer inside her mind and figure out what made her tick.

"For the show?" Tamera flipped the light on in the master bedroom. "It was shortly after that disaster of a date with Luke. I was feeling pretty crappy about myself and just wanted to get away. Landon heard about the open auditions on the radio and he and Julie drove me to them. They were worried I'd chicken out at the last minute."

Tamera seemed so confident and capable. Wyatt couldn't imagine her being afraid of anything. "And did you?"

"Almost," Tamera said, and he was surprised by the vulnerability he heard in her voice. "That date with Luke wasn't my finest moment. Letting the entire world see it was beyond humiliating. I was an internet meme for months. I was really worried that if I got on the show, I'd be the butt of everyone's jokes and emerge from the house to find that I'd made things a thousand times worse."

"But instead you changed everyone's opinions." He couldn't help but admire Tamera's tenacity.

"Yeah, I did. And now hopefully I can switch careers." She cleared her throat and pointed to the bay window on the far wall. "This room has a spectacular view. It's up high enough you can just see the ocean in the distance."

"It's beautiful." Wyatt stared at Tamera. The sunlight streamed in through the windows, softening her hair from a deep cappuccino to a warm caramel. He usually was attracted to women with long hair, but the shorter style fit her somehow. It was sassy, just like Tamera.

"You can easily fit a king-sized bed in here, along with a dresser and a couple of bedside tables." She walked through an archway and gasped. "Okay, if you don't buy this house, I will. This bathroom is to die for!"

Wyatt shook his head. What was he doing?

Tamera led him through the rest of the first floor. The other upstairs bedrooms would be perfect for his parents and sister to stay in when they visited, and the bathroom was large enough they wouldn't be fighting for space. Then Tamera led him downstairs, where he found a large game room that would hold his exercise equipment perfectly.

"Are you ready for the best part of the house?" Tamera asked. "I'm pretty sure you're going to love it, if the photos were any indication."

The movie room. It was part of what had made Wyatt want to see this house. "Let's check it out."

In the basement, two black double doors with gold handles stood at the end of a short hallway. Thick white crown molding framed the doorway, and above it the word *cinema* hung in block letters with lights in the center.

"Whoa," Wyatt said quietly.

Tamera opened one door, revealing a short hallway with red carpet and rope lights embedded in the floor. White wainscoting covered the bottom half of the wall on either side and movie posters hung on the walls.

"This is unreal," Wyatt said, padding the four paces down the hallway. He pivoted and sucked in a breath at the movie theater splayed before him.

Tamera clasped her hands together. "Brings a whole new meaning to the term *home theater*, huh? I'd sell a kidney for this room. Sunday movie marathons would be beyond amazing here."

"The pictures didn't do it justice." The room gradually descended in four steps, with four recliners on each row—enough to comfortably seat sixteen. A screen covered the entire wall. The dropped ceiling squares with hidden lighting probably made the acoustics in this room amazing.

Tamera walked across the back row and Wyatt followed. "The listing says ... yes, there."

A small alcove was cut into the room. A counter ran along the wall and a popcorn machine sat at one end. Shelves of candy clung to the wall, while a mini fridge hid underneath the counter.

"Not even my home in San Antonio had a theater this great." Wyatt had always meant to put one in, but hadn't gotten around to it. By the time that Becky left, and he started seriously considering a career in screenwriting again, it seemed pointless to put in the effort for a home he might not stay in much longer.

"I take it you like it?" Tamera asked.

He turned, surprised to find her so close in the dimly lit room. Her head barely reached his shoulders, despite wearing heels. He inhaled deeply and caught the faint aroma of strawberries from her shampoo.

"I love it."

"So we can move this to the maybe list?" He couldn't make out her features in the low lighting, but her voice sounded breathier than it had before.

"We can more than put this on the maybe list," Wyatt agreed, taking a step back. "I want to make an offer. All cash with a quick closing."

This wasn't happening. He couldn't be attracted to Tamera, the girl who'd begged him at three a.m. for a photo to share online. The girl who went on a date with a celebrity and ended up as an internet meme —and not in a good way. The girl who was friends with Drew Dempsey.

"Okay then," Tamera said. "Let's make it happen."

Wyatt nodded and left the theater room with one last, longing look. There was a magic in this room he definitely wanted to keep for himself.

Chapter Eleven

Tamera stayed up late writing the offer for Wyatt's house, then collapsed into bed and dreamed about him all night. When she awoke the next morning, she stretched languidly, feeling more relaxed than she had in months.

Wyatt was getting under her skin. For the first time since meeting him, that didn't seem like such a bad thing.

She went for a run, then showered and dressed before sitting down to read over the offer letter one last time. This was one of the biggest sales of her career, and only the third time she'd written an all-cash offer. It was definitely her first time working with a celebrity. She didn't want to make a mistake.

After only two small corrections, she deemed the letter perfect. Time to call Wyatt. Her fingers thrummed against her desk as the phone rang, the butterflies beating their wings in her stomach with every buzz.

"Hello?" Wyatt's deep, rich voice sent shivers down her spine, and Tamera's hand involuntarily curled into a fist.

"Hey. I just sent the offer letter to your email. Can you sign it electronically when you get a minute so I can submit it to the agent?"

"I've got time right now. Let me get to my computer." She heard the soft pad of feet, then a creak as he sat down in a chair. "Just booting up my laptop."

"I can wait." She twirled a lock of hair around one finger, unable to hide a grin. He could've said he'd get to it and hung up, but instead he kept her on the line.

"So, uh, were you serious about helping me out with the ad spots?"

"Yeah." Tamera ran a hand along the desk, telling herself to be cool.

"I think I'll take you up on your offer, then, if that's okay."

"Absolutely. Let's figure out a time that works for both of us." She wanted to beg him to come over right now. Go all fan-girl over Wyatt James. But it was more than the football player she was interested in. It was how his face lit up when he talked about a film he loved. The shy way he brushed off the spotlight. His uncanny ability to make her forget about everything except how much she enjoyed being around him.

"As long as it doesn't interfere with practice, I'll make anytime that's convenient for you work," Wyatt said.

She wanted to invite him over right now, but that might seem too eager. And she wasn't eager. Okay, maybe a little. "How about tomorrow night? Say, seven o'clock?"

"That's perfect."

"I'll text you my address."

"I really appreciate this, Tamera."

Was it her imagination, or did he linger over her name? Caress each vowel with his rough voice? She put a hand to her cheek and realized it was a few degrees warmer than typical.

Her emotions were getting out of hand.

"Okay, I've got the email. And ... signed. Emailing it back now."

"You don't want to read it over first?" Tamera asked.

"I trust you."

She shivered, her heart picking up its pace. She wanted to trust him, too. Drew's warnings seemed more and more ludicrous after each encounter with Wyatt.

A ping alerted her to a new email and she saw that Wyatt had indeed signed the offer. "Got it. I'll send this to the listing agent right now. Hopefully they accept without a counter-offer."

"Do you think it's likely they'll counter?"

"If it were me, I wouldn't counter. They're crazy if they think they'll get a better offer than full price and all cash. But it's really all up to the seller. We'll know soon enough."

"Yeah, I guess so. You'll let me know when you hear?"

"The very second," she promised him.

"Thanks."

A prolonged pause filled the line. Tamera pressed the phone closer to her ear, wishing she could see his expression right now. The silence zinged with emotions left unsaid. Whatever Drew had against Wyatt, it had to be an anomaly and not a character flaw. Because from where she was standing, Wyatt seemed Mary Poppins perfect.

"I guess I should let you go," Wyatt said finally. "You probably have work to do and I should get ready for practice."

"Yeah."

"Have a good day."

"You too," Tamera said.

Neither of them hung up. Could phones spontaneously ignite from heat? If so, hers was definitely in danger of going up in flames.

"Goodbye," Wyatt whispered. And then he finally hung up the phone.

"You're adorable," Tamera said to the empty line. She flung her phone onto the desk. "I'm insane to be thinking about you like this. You're severely testing my desire to remain forever single."

Her phone buzzed, skittering across the desk. Tamera nearly fell off her chair, but managed to save herself at the last moment and grabbed the phone. Had Wyatt somehow heard all of that? She would die of humiliation—

Why was Katie calling her?

She stared at the picture blazing across the call screen. It was from one of the last good days she'd had with Katie before finding out about the breakup. They'd gone to the beach, just the two of them, and spent the day working on their tans and laughing at the tourists. Tamera had gone to bed that night feeling better about their relationship than she had in years.

But Katie had been sleeping with Caleb for almost nine months by that point. And Tamera hadn't suspected a thing.

The phone went silent, then started ringing again almost immediately. Tamera picked it up with a growl. "What?"

"Hey," Katie said, her tone so sweet that Tamera felt her teeth spontaneously start to decay. "How are you doing?"

"How am I doing?" Tamera parroted back. Did Katie want to hear that she was still crying over the wedding?

Katie seemed to not even heard Tamera's response. "Things are so amazing here. I'm so not ready to go home tomorrow."

Tamera stayed silent. Because seriously, what was she supposed to say?

"You would absolutely adore the beaches," Katie continued. "I've never seen sand so white. It's so incredibly fine and soft, and the water is the bluest I've ever seen. We'll have to come back together someday. Caleb rented the cutest little bungalow you've ever seen. It's suspended on stilts over the water. Can you believe that? It's just crazy how picturesque everything is."

"Unbelievable," Tamera muttered.

"Excuse me?"

She pulled the phone away from her ear and spoke loudly directly into the receiver. "I said, you're unbelievable."

"I—"

But Tamera didn't let Katie speak. "You stole my groom, my wedding, and my honeymoon. The Bahamas is *my* dream destination— not yours. But that didn't stop you from taking it."

Katie's voice went from sugary to sour in an instant. "It's not like you have a monopoly on honeymoon destinations. We just wanted to get out of the cold for a while and enjoy warm sands."

"You live in Texas!" Tamera practically screamed into the phone. "It's May. The temperature was eighty-five degrees on your wedding day."

"Why can't you be happy for me?" Katie demanded, and she had the pout in her voice that had always turned their parents to spineless jellyfish. "I just got married—*married*, Tamera. I made the biggest commitment of my life. And you've been nothing but negative and unsupportive from the very beginning."

"Maybe you shouldn't have made that commitment because of some ridiculous vendetta you have against me."

"Maybe you shouldn't have always taken what was mine!" Katie screamed.

Tamera yanked the phone away, her ear ringing with the intensity of the words. Silence fell between them, thick and uncomfortable.

"I'm sorry I've made you so miserable," Tamera said finally, bitterness edging each word. "I'm sorry I let you be that obnoxious little sister who always hung out with me and my friends. I'm sorry I taught you how to put on makeup and do your hair. I'm sorry for trying to be a good sister, because all that got me was a very large knife right in my back."

"I was constantly competing against you," Katie said. "It didn't matter what I did, because you'd already done it better. Grades. Extracurriculars. Guys."

"So your solution was to sleep with my boyfriend behind my back, then marry him?"

Silence stretched across the line and Tamera blinked, forcing the tears to finally spill down her cheeks. "Have a nice life, Katie."

"Tamera—"

She hung up the phone, then dropped her head to her arms and cried.

Chapter Twelve

"She's in my head, Nat." Wyatt lay on the creaky hotel bed and tossed the football straight into the air, then caught it with one hand. His other loosely held the telephone to one ear. "Asking for her help with the commercial was a very bad idea."

"Why?" Natalie asked. "You suck at acting. Without her help, you'll probably hurt the team more than you help it. People will be like, 'Wow, that Wyatt James is a total drag. No way I'm going to see him play.'"

"Thanks," Wyatt said dryly. "What would I do without your undying support?"

"You know I'm right. You're a train wreck on camera. Makes me seriously question if Luke Ryder really is as business savvy as everyone claims. Maybe the conspiracy theorists are right—his father really was cryogenically preserved and is leading the company from the grave."

"That's ridiculous."

"Wyatt." Natalie was using her mother hen tone now—the one that had always driven Wyatt insane, especially since she was the younger sister. "There is no denying that Becky was a completely selfish harpy. But that doesn't mean all women are like her. If you like Tamera, ask her out. Maybe, after a few dates, you'll decide she's not someone you want a relationship with. But maybe you'll finally discover everything you've always wanted."

"Wow. That was cheesy, even for you."

"Maybe it's cheesy, but it's also the truth. What is it about Tamera that has you running away with your tail between your legs?"

There was a pull between the two of them that Wyatt couldn't describe, and it was that something he couldn't put into words that freaked him out more than anything. "She's an actress, for starters."

"Yeah, I watched *Eye in the Sky*."

"Actresses are shallow and vain."

"So are football players, and yet somehow you're still a pretty decent guy."

Wyatt tossed the football into the air again and let out a frustrated sigh. "She's friends with Drew. And if she thinks he's a good guy, that pretty much tells me all I need to know."

"You're being an idiot."

Wyatt flinched. "Ouch."

"Well, it's true. Sometimes people are poor judges of character. Look at you and Becky. She turned out to be a total Medusa, but that doesn't make you a bad person for dating her."

It didn't make him a good person, either. He ran his finger along the stitching of the football, feeling like such a girl for talking to his sister about his relationship problems. "Tamera can help me with my acting, we'll close on the house, and then I never have to see her again."

"Yeah, that sounds like an incredibly mature way to deal with this whole thing. Just shove your feelings down and pretend they don't exist. That'll show Becky."

"Low blow," Wyatt grumbled.

"I call it like I see it."

Wyatt knew she was right, which bothered him more than anything else. He'd been unfair to Tamera since the very beginning, judging her based on a criteria she'd had no part in creating.

"Nothing stings as bad as regret," Natalie said.

"You sound like Dad."

"He's a smart guy."

Wyatt said nothing.

Natalie sighed dramatically. "Sheesh, Wyatt. This isn't rocket science. Just ask Tamera out. No matter how the date ends, at least you won't wonder what could've happened if you'd stopped being a pansy and actually tried."

"I'm not being a pansy." But the protest sounded half-hearted, even to him. Wyatt glanced at his watch, then sat up. "I've got to go, Nat. Don't want to be late for practice."

"Man up and take her out, okay? For me, if for no one else. I can't listen to you whine about this for too much longer before I lose my mind."

"Thanks for the support."

She laughed. "Love you."

"Love you, too."

Wyatt couldn't stop thinking about his conversation with Natalie as he drove to the stadium. Maybe she was right, and he should ask Tamera out. They'd never really spent time together outside of house hunting and that one awkward first meeting at the gym. Maybe if they hung out more outside of work, he'd discover she wasn't all that interesting after all.

Yeah. Maybe he'd be traded back to the Vigilantes next season, too.

In the locker room, Wyatt chatted with Tyrone while they got ready for practice. When they headed onto the field, they were surprised to see Luke waiting with McKinley for them.

"Think this is good?" Tyrone muttered out of the corner of his mouth.

Wyatt stared at Luke. The man's posture was relaxed, his hands in his pockets and a lazy smile on his lips. "Doesn't look bad at least."

A few minutes later, the rest of the team was on the field and McKinley raised his hand. The players quickly quieted down and gave the coach their full attention.

"Our owner, Mr. Ryder, has asked to speak with us all for a few minutes before practice," McKinley said. "Whenever you're ready, Mr. Ryder."

Luke stepped forward. "I'll just take a minute of your time," he said.

"Ryder Communications, in partnership with Footsteps for Change, a community outreach program we frequently work with, is doing a special one-day event at Universal Studios a week from Saturday. We're giving free tickets to at-risk youth and their families so they can enjoy a day bonding with each other, away from their problems. McKinley and I discussed it, and we think this is a great opportunity for the team to give back. We'd like to invite all players and their families to join us for the event. Footsteps for Change will organize meet-and-greets around the park where the kids can get autographs and photos with the players. We'll get the specifics out to you soon, but I'd like to personally encourage all of you to attend this event with your families. We can do some good for the community and rack up some positive press for the team in the process."

"Everyone will be there," McKinley said, clapping Luke on the back. "We really appreciate the opportunity."

"It'll be a fun day, I think," Luke said. "My wife is also organizing a gender reveal party for the press. It'll be another good PR opportunity for the team."

Gender reveal? Wyatt scratched the back of his neck. Like a floofy party to say whether the baby was a boy or girl?

Luke raised a hand in farewell. "I'm heading back to the office. Any questions can be directed to the team press liaison. She knows where to find me."

McKinley folded his arms across his massive chest and watched Mr. Ryder leave the stadium. The team stayed quiet, watching the coach watch Luke leave.

"Right," McKinley said once Luke had disappeared around the corner. "I know Mr. Ryder said this was an invitation, but I'm making it mandatory for all players to attend. Anyone who doesn't show up will be doing sprints up the bleachers during every practice for a solid week. Understood?"

A rumble of assent echoed back. It wasn't like this event would cut into Wyatt's social schedule any. It sounded fun. He'd never been to Universal Studios, and he'd always enjoyed meet-and-greets with younger fans the best.

Maybe he'd invite Tamera to join him for the day. With her interest in acting, she probably enjoy Universal Studios. Maybe, like him, she'd never been there before.

He'd ask her when they met tonight.

Chapter Thirteen

Tamera hung up with the listing agent, a big grin on her face. They'd accepted Wyatt's offer on the house and she couldn't wait to tell him.

Her fingers fumbled to bring up his contact information. He'd be at her house in just a few hours so they could work on his camera presence, but this was the kind of information that she couldn't hold onto for even a minute.

"Hey, Tamera." Wyatt's deep voice had the hair on her arms standing on end, even across the phone line.

"I've got some exciting news for you," she said, unable to keep a squeal from her voice. "They accepted your offer on the house! We close in two weeks as long as nothing unexpected shows up in the inspection."

"That's awesome." The enthusiasm in his voice was contagious. "You have no idea how happy this makes me."

"Sick of the hotel?" she teased.

"That's the understatement of the century. I can't wait to finally get settled."

A warm silence filtered through the line, crackling with chemistry.

Tamera clutched the phone tight, her stomach swarming with butterflies she could no longer even attempt to squelch.

"We'll have to celebrate when you come over tonight," she ventured. "Let me feed you dinner."

"Dinner sounds great."

"Any special dietary restrictions I should be aware of?" She knew from the summer spent with Drew that the team nutritionists were pretty strict with their requirements.

"More than I can even begin to explain. Let me bring dinner to you."

"Well now I feel silly."

His deep, rich laugh had her entire body tingling with awareness. "Don't. I'll see you at seven."

"Seven," she agreed, and hung up the line.

The next few hours went by at a glacial pace. Tamera traded emails back and forth with another agent for almost an hour, then tried to practice her lines for an upcoming audition. A few new home listings came through, and she sent her recommendations to a few of her clients, along with a few of Landon's. Julie was still pretty sick, and while the baby was fine, it looked like she might be stuck in the hospital for a while.

At four o'clock, Tamera shut down her laptop and started getting ready for Wyatt. She took a long, hot shower and spent her time straightening her hair until it was sleek and soft. Then she expertly applied her makeup, trying to ignore the way her hands shook as she held the various brushes and wands.

Tonight wasn't a date. It wasn't even kind of a date. She was celebrating an offer acceptance with a client and giving him a few pointers on acting so that he didn't feel so uncomfortable in front of the camera. The fact she'd never done anything like this for any other client was beside the point.

She slipped into her softest pair of jeans and her favorite blouse, then worked on straightening up her condo. She'd loved the white couch and gray tiled fireplace when she bought the place, but they suddenly looked woefully inadequate compared to the home Wyatt was buying. Sure, it wasn't anywhere close to the opulent mansion he could probably afford. But his new home, with the open spaces and to-die-for movie room, was mountains above her small two-bedroom condo.

He's not Caleb, she reminded herself. Her ex-boyfriend—brother-in-law—whatever he was—had certainly thought investing in a condo was a waste of money. He didn't understand why she wanted to buy something so small instead of waiting until she could afford something bigger.

"Don't be stupid," she said aloud. Wyatt wasn't like that.

But Drew's warning played at the back of her mind.

A knock echoed through the condo and sent Tamera's heart racing. She took a deep breath and smoothed down the front of her blouse, then cast one last look around her condo. In the kitchen, the sink was free of dishes and the quartz counters were wiped clean. She'd arranged the orange and teal throw pillows—the only pop of color in the room—on the couch. She'd dusted the fireplace mantle.

It was as good as it was going to get.

She walked to the front door on trembling legs and opened it. Her pulse nearly flat-lined at the sight of Wyatt. A ball cap shadowed his face and one hand was shoved in the pocket of his dark denim jeans. A blue T-shirt strained against his muscles, and she caught the faintest whiff of his aftershave.

"Hey," she said, leaning against the door for support.

He tugged at the brim of his ball cap, a soft smile quirking up the edge of his mouth. He held up a grocery bag and for the first time her brain registered the delicious aroma coming from it. "I brought dinner."

"Great. Come in." She stepped aside, trying not to stare at his backside as he sauntered in.

Drew was insane. There was clearly nothing wrong with Wyatt James. Not a darn thing.

"You can set it on the table," she said, motioning to the square black table big enough to seat four.

"Cool." He lifted plastic containers from the bag. "I hope you aren't a vegetarian. My nutritionist made grilled chicken."

"Definitely not a vegetarian. It smells delicious."

He pulled off his ball cap and set it on the couch, and her heart flipped. "You lucked out. My nutritionist in San Antonio didn't worry much about taste. I'm definitely eating much better in California than I ever was in Texas."

"Good, because I'm not a football player and I refuse to eat anything that tastes like dirt."

He laughed and the sound seemed to fill her entire condo. She hadn't realized how cold the place had felt before. His warmth seemed to encompass every inch of the place.

She opened a cupboard and pulled out two glasses, feeling suddenly shy. She motioned to the bottle of wine open on the counter. "I thought tonight was cause for celebrating."

His eyes glinted as he watched her pour two glasses. "No complaints from me."

She brought the glasses over to the table and sat one in front of him. The next few minutes were filled with idle chatter as they filled their plates and dug in.

Tamera pointed to her chicken. "This is really good."

"Don't act so surprised."

"Well, you spoke so highly of your last nutritionist."

Wyatt laughed. "Maybe the team in Texas just really hated me, so they gave me the worst chef."

Tamera cocked her head to the side, watching Wyatt contemplatively. The words were flippant, but there was an undercurrent of something that she wasn't quite sure how to decipher.

"Were things hard for you in Texas?"

He took a bite of his chicken and chewed slowly, as though giving himself time to think. "Unexpected complications arose," he said finally.

"What kinds of complications?"

He wouldn't meet her eyes, and that knot was back in her stomach —the knot that Drew had put there with his suggestion that Wyatt wasn't all that he seemed. "Nothing worth mentioning. I wasn't sure about the trade to the Coyotes at first, but I'm really enjoying California." He held her eyes. "Really enjoying it."

She sucked in a breath and focused on her food. "You'll be enjoying it a lot more in about two weeks, when you're living in your own home again. What are you going to do to the movie room?"

"Not much. It's practically perfect the way it is."

"Yeah, it's pretty amazing."

"You'll have to come over for its inaugural showing."

Had he just asked her out? She looked at the food spread before them and wondered if he considered this a date. Did she want him to?

"Sounds like fun." She took a bite of her salad. She needed to focus. "So, how did things go with the team today?"

"Great. We're doing a team event at Universal Studios a week from Saturday. Ryder Communications has partnered with a charity that's bringing in at-risk kids."

"I've always wanted to go to Universal Studios." Tamera took another bite of her food.

"You've never been?"

She shook her head and laughed. "People come from all over the world to see it, but I live fifteen miles away and have never been."

"You should come with me." He focused on his food, not looking at her.

Her heart skipped a beat. "Really?"

"Mr. Ryder told us to bring family and friends." He shrugged. "It'll be fun to experience the park with someone who appreciates film as much as I do."

"In that case, I accept."

What was she doing? Working with Wyatt was one thing, but this was definitely entering friendship—possibly dating—territory.

"Awesome." He glanced up and shot her a quick grin. "It's going to be a lot of fun."

"I think so, too."

She cleared her throat and looked away. *Focus, Tamera.* Her heart couldn't keep going aflutter every time they were together. He was here to learn about acting, not to flirt. She was like eighty percent sure of that. "So did you shoot any more commercials today?"

"Thankfully no. If I have another shoot as bad as the last two, I'm pretty sure Mr. Ryder is going to rethink his request that I be in them. Maybe that's not such a bad thing."

"Come on. You can't be that bad."

He raised an eyebrow. "Want to bet?"

She laughed, taking a final bite of her salad and then pushing her mostly-empty plate away. Wyatt's plate was empty and they'd both drained their wine glasses. "Show me what you've got."

"Seriously?"

"I can't help you until I know what I'm dealing with." She motioned to the living room. "Pretend you're on set and doing a take."

"Okay." He pushed back from the table and stood in the middle of her living room. He cleared his throat and shifted from foot to foot. "It's really awful."

Tamera folded her arms and rolled her eyes. "Stop stalling. I'm here to help, not judge."

"Okay. Okay." He shook out his hands and she hid a grin by pretending to scratch her nose.

"You can do it," Tamera encouraged.

"I'm usually holding a football."

"Just pretend you've got one in your hand."

"Right." He took a deep breath, and then a grimace crossed his face. Wait. Was that supposed to be a smile?

He took a step forward, his hand held out in front of him in an awkward cupping motion. Was that how he held an actual football on set? She knew for a fact it wasn't how he held one on the field.

"Hi," he said, his voice a painfully loud monotone. "I'm Wyatt James an offensive lineman for the Los Angeles Coyotes you've probably seen me play on television or maybe even been to a game."

He didn't pause for breath—added absolutely no punctuation to his sentences. It all came out in a rush, said at the exact same speed.

He took a step forward, then paused. "This year the Coyotes are bigger and better than ever we have new players a new coach and a new owner we're basically a brand new team and we want to invite you to be a part of it."

Tamera couldn't help it. A giggle burst forth and she made a slicing motion across her neck with one finger. "Cut."

His hand dropped to his side and pink tinged his cheeks. "Told you I was bad."

"I thought you were exaggerating."

He ran a hand over his head. "I'm fine playing on the field. But this kind of thing is totally outside my ability."

"It's not." She walked over to him and placed a hand on each of his arms. She stared up into his eyes, trying to ignore the frantic beating of her heart. "Don't think of it as a camera. Think of it as talking to a fan. One single fan. Pretend you're talking to me."

His lips curved up in a smile. "You're one of my fans?"

She dropped her hands and took a step away. "You know I love football."

Mischief glinted in his eyes, but he nodded. "Of course."

"First of all, you need to loosen up." She rolled her shoulders back and stretched her neck. "Come on—do it."

He rolled his shoulders, looking as stiff as a board. Tamera leaned over, resting her hands on her legs as laughter shook her body.

"That's how you relax?" she gasped.

Wyatt threw up his hands. "It's hopeless."

"Stop." She rested her hands on his biceps and his breathing stilled. Slowly, she ran her hands down his arms. The muscles were like stone beneath her light touch. She reached his hands and curled her fingers through his. He responded by closing his hands tightly around hers and taking a step closer.

"Now what?" he breathed.

Slowly, she raised their hands up in the air and then out to their sides. "Pretend your limbs are liquid. Imagine a waterfall is pouring over you."

He let her guide his hands, up and out, down to their sides, back up. Then he took control, bringing her hands to rest against his chest.

"Feel relaxed?" she whispered.

He captured both her hands in one of his, trapping them against his chest. She could feel his heart beating frantically underneath her palms as he brushed a strand of hair behind her cheek.

"Completely," he breathed.

She pressed herself tighter against him, an involuntary reaction to the caress of his fingers on her cheeks. His large hand made its way to the back of her neck and she rose on her tiptoes.

A knock echoed through the condo, shattering the moment. Tamera jumped away and Wyatt's hands dropped to his side. She stared at the door, her chest heaving with what had almost just happened.

Wyatt cleared his throat and ran a hand over his chin. "Are you expecting visitors?"

"No. It's probably just a neighbor wanting to borrow an egg or something." She walked to the door, trying not to stumble like a love-drunk idiot.

She'd almost kissed Wyatt James. Her body felt flushed with heat and she pressed a hand to her cheek. Definitely warm from a blush. She was supposed to be helping Wyatt with his acting, not almost kissing him.

She peered through the peephole, then gasped.

Wyatt took a step forward, his posture going rigid as though he was prepared to protect if necessary. "Who is it?"

She shook her head and motioned with one hand for him to relax. "It's only Drew."

"What?" Wyatt's single word was harsh and filled with something she couldn't put her finger on.

"I had no idea he was in town," Tamera said, feeling her stomach coil with nerves. Two parts of her life that didn't like each other were about to collide, and she wasn't eager for the explosion.

"Come on, Tamera," Drew said on the other side of the door. "I can hear you in there. Let me in."

"Sorry," Tamera mouthed at Wyatt. His jaw was clenched, his eyes dark. Then she unlocked the door, pasting a smile on her lips. "Hey, Drew."

He laughed, lifting her off the ground with a giant bear hug. "It's good to see you."

"What are you doing in town?"

"You sounded so upset when we talked last that I decided to hop on a plane." Drew set her down, looking over the top of her head into the condo, and stiffened. She knew he'd seen Wyatt.

Tamera cleared her throat and stepped back, letting Drew inside. "I guess you two know each other."

She looked back and forth between the two men. They faced off like two bulls in a pen, their tightly corded muscles straining their T-shirts with tension. Both men had their jaws clenched and their arms tightly folded across massive chests. For a moment, she had the urge to push

Drew backward out of the condo and lock the door so she and Wyatt could go back to the easy chemistry that had sizzled between them moments before. She'd really been looking forward to that kiss.

"I'd better get going," Wyatt said. He grabbed his ball cap off the couch and nodded to Tamera. "Thanks for your help tonight."

"You don't have to go," Tamera said even as she walked him to the door.

"Yeah, I think I do." Wyatt glanced at Drew, then leaned down and gave Tamera a tight hug. "Don't believe a word he says," he whispered in her ear.

Tamera stepped back, her mind swirling with confusion.

Wyatt gave a quick nod, then disappeared down the hallway. Tamera shut the door, turned to Drew, and folded her arms.

"You've got a lot of explaining to do," she said. "Start talking."

Chapter Fourteen

◈

Drew motioned to Tamera's white couch, his expression serious. "Can we sit?"

She ran a hand through her hair, then blew out a breath. Why was he here? "Yeah. Sounds like this might take a while."

Drew nodded and sank into the cushion. She could almost hear it groan under his weight. He looked comical, like a baby doll trying to sit on a couch made for Barbies. Wyatt and Drew were roughly the same size, but somehow Wyatt had looked like he belonged in her living room while Drew looked decidedly out of place.

Tamera sank into the chair across from him, wanting a little distance. "I wasn't expecting to see you tonight."

"I could tell how much the texts from Caleb were messing with you. I wanted to help if I could."

His words touched her heart, easing the frustration she felt over the interrupted kiss. Tamera rested a hand on his arm. "Thanks for looking out for me."

He covered her hand with his, but it felt like a trap instead of a comfort. When he looked at her, she saw something in his eyes she hadn't noticed before. Desire.

She yanked her hand back, startled. Drew always flirted, but was it possible he actually meant it?

"What was Wyatt doing here?" Drew demanded.

Tamera looked away. "I can't tell you."

His eyes bulged and he clenched his hands into fists, resting them on his knees. "What do you mean you can't tell me?"

"I signed a nondisclosure."

"So you're working for him." It wasn't a question.

"You know I can't confirm or deny that."

"Tonight looked like a lot more than a work meeting." Drew leaned back, smashing her orange and teal throw pillows flat beneath his bulk. He gestured to the table, where their empty wine glasses and plates still sat. "Dinner. Wine. Sounds like a date."

"It wasn't," Tamera said, unable to keep the defensive edge from her voice. She and Drew were just friends. Not even best friends. He didn't get to comment on her love life.

"Did you want it to be?"

Tamera ran a shaky hand through her hair, thinking of the way her entire body had yearned for that almost-kiss. She'd leaned into Wyatt. Practically begged his lips to capture hers. "I don't know."

Drew swore. "I warned you about him, Tamera. Stay away."

"What's so bad about Wyatt?" Tamera threw out her arms. "I've spent a lot of time with him over the past two weeks, and I honestly don't know what made you warn me to stay away."

"He's a snake."

"He's kind," Tamera shot back. "He's humble and chivalrous. He makes me laugh."

"So does a cat video. That doesn't mean you should date it."

"We're not dating." She rose and began to pace, then stopped in front of Drew. "Why shouldn't I date him?"

Drew's jaw twitched. "I told you to trust me."

"I do." Well, she trusted him like ninety percent. Maybe eighty. She sank onto the couch next to Drew. "Trust isn't enough. I really like Wyatt. If you honesty believe I shouldn't date him, then I need to know what he did that was so awful."

Drew raised a hand and rubbed at his shoulder, as though his injury from last season was bothering him again. "Wyatt and I weren't exactly friends in San Antonio," he said finally. "But we weren't enemies, either. Not at first. We weren't really anything. We worked together on the field, but that was it."

If Drew had been keeping her from Wyatt over a vague dislike with no solid basis, she was going to kill him. "And that means I shouldn't date him?"

Drew shot her a look. "Are you going to let me tell the story or not?"

"Sorry." She pantomimed locking her lips and throwing away the key. She wanted to hear this story so badly it had her legs trembling.

Wyatt is a good guy, she repeated over and over in her head. Whatever Drew said, it wouldn't change that. Right?

"Wyatt dated a girl for a while," Drew said finally. "Becky."

"The cheerleader he broke up with," Tamera said, remembering the one small article she'd read on the subject. It hadn't given a lot of information—just mentioned the couple had been dating, but Becky had cheated.

Drew nodded. "Yeah. The cheerleaders don't usually spend a lot of time with the team outside of games and maybe a few parties. But Becky started hanging around more and more once she and Wyatt started dating. Before too long, she started coming onto me. I tried to put her off. I mean, she was Wyatt's girlfriend. But she cornered me in the locker room one day and kissed me. Wyatt walked in before I could push her away and was furious."

Tamera rubbed her temples, trying to process what Drew had just told her. "He thought you were having an affair with Becky."

"I couldn't really blame the guy." Drew blew out a breath. "I tried to talk to him, but he wasn't interested in hearing it. Becky was sobbing and saying she'd made a mistake, but Wyatt wouldn't listen to her. He told her they were over. It was so cold. Like she meant nothing to him."

"He'd just found out his girlfriend was cheating on him," Tamera said hotly. She folded her arms, feeling her skin flush as she jumped to Wyatt's defense. "That kind of thing hits you like a ton of bricks. It isn't easy to control your reaction in the heat of the moment. I should know."

"Shhh." Drew grabbed her hand and pulled her toward him, forcing her head to rest on his chest. She resisted at first, but finally relented when his hands started playing with her hair. "I'm not trying to bag on Wyatt. I felt just as bad about the whole situation as he did. But then Becky wouldn't leave me alone."

Prickles of unease had Tamera feeling a little queasy. "How so?"

"She kept calling me, showing up at my house, that sort of thing. Somehow Wyatt found out. Maybe Becky told him—I think she was still trying to get him back. I don't know. But from that point forward, it seemed like Wyatt's mission in life was to ruin my career."

The words sank in, and the queasy feeling in Tamera's stomach hardened into a rock. She pushed away from Drew, shaking her head. "No. That doesn't sound like Wyatt."

"I wouldn't have believed it either if I wasn't there. Maybe we weren't friends, but I always thought he was one of the good guys."

Tamera rose and began pacing again. She ran a hand through her hair, imagining the way Wyatt's deep brown eyes pulled her in and made her want to stay near him forever. She shook her head again, this time more frantically. "He wouldn't ruin your career because his girlfriend was awful."

Drew leaned back against the couch, watching her with his sky blue eyes. "You can't ignore the facts, Tamera. Wyatt started slacking at practice. At first, I thought he was distracted because of the breakup. Things like that sometimes mess with a guy's focus. But a few weeks passed and nothing improved. I started noticing he deliberately wasn't protecting me from getting sacked."

"No." Tamera put a hand to her heart, feeling it twist.

"Wyatt's the reason I got hurt last season." Drew rose, and there was a fire in his eyes she'd glimpsed a time or two while they were playing *Eye in the Sky*. "He deliberately left me open and my throwing arm got damaged as a result. Coach saw what was happening as clear as day, and told Wyatt he could either be traded at the end of the season or he'd take what he knew to the press."

Tamera blinked back the tears forming behind her eyes. "He wouldn't do that. This has got to be some sort of crazy misunderstanding. Did you actually talk to him after you got hurt?"

"I knew there wasn't a point. He was so angry, and the damage had already been done."

Red flags were waving frantically in Tamera's head, but she didn't know whether or not to trust them. Was Drew's version of events actually false, or did she just want Wyatt to be good that badly? Drew wouldn't lie to her, but sometimes perception wasn't quite the same as reality.

Drew scratched the back of his head. "That was a really hard time for me. You actually helped me a lot on *Eye in the Sky*. Hanging out with you felt so normal."

Tamera snorted. "Nothing about reality television is normal."

"You know what I mean." Drew nudged her arm, sending her a flirty grin. "I wasn't sure if I'd ever play again. The uncertainty was killing me. But then I met you, and we had so much fun together."

Okay, they were venturing into territory Tamera didn't even want to put a toe in. "So you knew the coach was blackmailing Wyatt into a trade?"

Drew scowled. "It was a generous offer. Coach could've ended Wyatt's career, but he didn't."

"The Coyotes are a huge step back and you know it."

"You don't know what it's like to be part of a team," Drew shot back. "Coach asked me to keep quiet, so I did. Wyatt was transferred to the Coyotes and that was that."

She couldn't be falling for another guy who'd fooled her into thinking he was something he wasn't. "No. There's got to be more to the story."

"Tamera." Drew grabbed her arms, forcing her to stop pacing. His touch was gentle, but firm. "Think about it. Why else would Wyatt trade from a team with a shot at the championships to a team that's probably not even going to make the playoffs?"

Tamera had had similar thoughts when she first found out about the trade. In some twisted way, Drew was making sense. A tear fell and she quickly brushed it away. She folded her arms and looked at the ground, not wanting to meet Drew's eyes. "I really liked him."

Drew pulled her to him. He was bigger even than Wyatt and her arms barely fit around his waist. She blinked again, but all it did was make more tears fall onto Drew's shirt. He wrapped his arms around her and she closed her eyes. Why couldn't she be attracted to Drew in a romantic way? He was such a good friend and seemed interested in pursuing more. But her feelings had never been more than platonic.

"I'm sorry," he said, kissing the top of her head. "I should've told you from the beginning. But Coach asked me to keep everything quiet. He was worried that the story would negatively impact the Vigilantes if it got out. Now that Wyatt's been traded, I don't want to throw mud at each other in the press. That'll hurt me just as much as it'll hurt him. I just want to move on and forget the whole thing ever happened"

"I won't tell anyone," Tamera whispered.

Drew rested his head on the top of hers. "I know you won't."

They stood there for a moment while Tamera tried to wrap her head around this new information. She'd been so wrong about Wyatt. At this rate, she'd never be able to trust her feelings.

"Come on." Drew pulled away. "I'm taking you out on the town tonight. You need some fun."

Tamera forced a smile. "Sounds great. Let me freshen up a bit and then we can go."

Drew nodded and Tamera escaped to the solitude of her bedroom. She sank against her closed door and slid to the floor.

How could she have been so wrong?

Chapter Fifteen

Drew was once again trying to ruin Wyatt's life. He stared at the ceiling of his hotel room for hours, failing spectacularly at keeping Tamera from his mind.

When Drew had showed up at Tamera's condo, Wyatt felt like he'd been punched in the gut. The air had escaped him in a whoosh of despair. No doubt Drew had stayed at Tamera's condo for hours, telling his side of the story. Scratch that. *Lying* about his side of the story.

Why couldn't he have waited two minutes to show up? Wyatt was pretty sure he'd been about to experience an earth-shattering kiss with Tamera. He desperately wanted a second chance at that particular moment. But Drew would try his hardest to poison Tamera's mind.

At five o'clock, Wyatt finally gave up trying to sleep on the too-hard hotel mattress and got up. Two weeks and he'd be sleeping on his own bed again, in his own home. Somehow the excitement of his offer being accepted had been dashed by Drew's arrival. Worse yet, Wyatt hadn't gotten help with his clearly atrocious acting. He'd really needed that help.

Since it was Saturday, there was no team practice. Wyatt tried to keep busy by lifting weights in the hotel gym, then running ten miles. He talked to Natalie on the phone for a while and wrote a few scenes for his latest script, then headed to the movies alone just to have something to do.

The action movie was weak at best, relying more on special effects and scantily clad women than an actual storyline. Wyatt's attention drifted in the dark theater. Had Drew headed back to Texas, or was he spending the day with Tamera? Was he staying at her condo or at a hotel? One thing was certain—Drew was interested in Tamera as more than a friend. Wyatt had recognized the predatory glint in his nemesis's eyes. He just hoped Tamera could see through it.

His thoughts continued to consume him as he drove back to the hotel after the film. The congested California traffic had him gritting his teeth as he crept along the freeway inch by inch. Yet another strike against Drew. In that moment, Wyatt missed Texas so badly it took his breath away.

"You've received a new text from Tyrone," Talia said, her voice filling the cab of his truck. "Would you like me to read it to you?"

"Sure," Wyatt said, clutching at the outside interaction like a lifeline. Maybe Tyrone would invite him over to hang out. Anything would be better than this crushing loneliness.

"Party at Schroeder's tonight," Talia read. "Can pick you up in ten."

Ugh. Next time, Wyatt would be more careful what he wished for, because another silent evening spent alone in his hotel room sounded a thousand times more appealing than suffering through another one of Schroeder's mindless parties. Wyatt had only attended one so far, but he had a feeling they were all the same—lots of booze and lots of women. But failing to make an appearance would create waves in waters Wyatt would rather remain still.

"Send a reply," he said.

"Okay. What should I say?" Talia asked.

"On my way back to the hotel now. See you in a few."

"Sent," Talia said.

Wyatt nodded and gripped the steering wheel, feeling his pent-up frustrations pulse through him. Until yesterday, he'd still been half-convinced that staying away from Tamera was the right decision. But then his conversation with Natalie had messed with his head and he'd almost kissed Tamera instead. Now he ... what? Wanted to see where things went with Tamera? Wanted to officially date her?

"You're an idiot," he muttered to himself as he pulled into the hotel parking lot. Drew had probably done him a favor by showing up and stopping the kiss.

Wyatt recognized Tyrone's sleek silver Maserati immediately, straddling two parking spaces near the back of the lot. The designer vehicle looked decidedly out of place among the minivans and economy cars of the other hotel guests. Wyatt parked a stall away from Tyrone— no sense tempting fate by parking close enough to potentially scratch Tyrone's paint job—and jumped out of his truck.

"Thanks for driving," Wyatt said as he climbed into the car. He settled back against the rich leather and barely held back a sigh of satisfaction. He couldn't deny that luxury cars were a dream to ride in, even if they did cost as much as a house.

"No problem, man. Where you coming from?"

"The movie theater."

"By yourself?"

Wyatt shrugged. "There's not much to do at the hotel. I was ready to get out for a while."

Tyrone nodded as he pulled out of the parking lot. "Any luck house hunting?"

"Yeah, actually. I just had an offer accepted yesterday."

"Congrats. We'll have to do a housewarming party to christen the place."

"Definitely," Wyatt agreed. Nothing sounded less fun, but he didn't want the team to perceive him as snobbish or anything. Maybe Tamera would have some ideas on how to make the party great. Natalie would want to make suggestions for the food, obviously, but Tamera seemed like the type who played hostess well. He could almost imagine her laughing with Tyrone and the other guys as she sat on his living room couch. Would it be weird to ask for her help? He wasn't sure where they stood at the moment. His phone burned in his pocket, tempting him to call her and find out, but he thought giving her space this weekend was probably the wisest course of action.

Tyrone waved a hand in front of Wyatt's face. "Anyone home?"

Wyatt blinked. "Yeah. Sorry."

Tyrone grinned knowingly. "It's a girl, ain't it? Only a woman can make a man look that stupid."

Wyatt shifted uncomfortably. He didn't want anyone on the Coyotes to know about his history with Drew. "Maybe."

"What's her name?" Tyrone prodded.

If he tried to keep it secret, that would only make Tyrone more curious. "Tamera. She's my real estate agent, but we hung out last night. She's an aspiring actress and offered to help me with the stupid commercial spot."

"She must like you, too. Pretty sure acting class isn't in her job description as a real estate agent."

"It's complicated."

Tyrone snorted as he revved the engine and darted between two cars. "You like her. She likes you. Doesn't sound that complicated to me, bro."

"Did you hear the part where she's my real estate agent."

Tyrone waved a had dismissively. "Only for a few more weeks. That's a weak excuse and you know it."

It was only two weeks until he closed on the house. Wyatt really hoped they wouldn't be awkward and tense. He had no idea what to expect the next time he and Tamera spoke. Drew had told his side of the story. Anything Wyatt said would just seem like a lie. Of course Tamera would be more inclined to believe the friend she'd lived with in a glass house for twelve weeks over the acquaintance she barely knew.

The conversation switched to discussing the team's last few practices as they made their way toward Schroeder's beachside mansion in Malibu. Tyrone slowed as they approached the gates and after three security checkpoints they pulled into the driveway.

Schroeder's home boasted an impressive outdoor living space and enough land between him and the neighbors that no one would complain about the loud music that pulsed out of the home. The driveway was already crowded with BMWs and Mercedes, but Tyrone found an open spot and parked with a sigh.

"Let's get this over with," Tyrone said.

"Took the words right out of my mouth." Wyatt tapped his index finger against one leg. "What's the deal with guys like Schroeder? We should be able to skip a party without declaring war."

"You know how it is, man. The quarterback owns us. That's how it's been on every team since high school."

Wyatt got out of the car with a snort. Drew had certainly called all the shots in San Antonio. He was still calling the shots. Wyatt knew that for most of the guys on the Coyotes, the almost weekly parties at Schroeder's were a benefit of the team. But Wyatt could already tell he was going to hate them.

Tyrone pushed open Schroeder's massive front door without knocking. Music played at a decibel that nearly shattered Wyatt's eardrums, but no one in the crowded entryway seemed to notice or care.

Wyatt gave a few of the guys fist bumps as he and Tyrone pushed their way toward the main area of the house. Schroeder sat in the living room, blonde twigs with surgically enhanced bosoms nuzzling him on either side.

"Hey!" Schroeder raised a hand toward them, a stupid grin on his face.

Wyatt raised a hand as well, consciously willing himself not to scowl. Schroeder's arrogance reminded him so much of Drew. The similarities made it hard not to dislike the guy on principle.

"Drinks in the kitchen," Schroeder said. "Help yourself. The hot tub and pool are open outside, and the game room's downstairs."

"Thanks, man," Tyrone said. He nodded his head toward the kitchen and Wyatt gratefully followed him out of the room.

In the kitchen, soda cans and beer bottles rested in troughs filled with ice that ran the length of the counter. The nutritionists would be apoplectic if they saw this spread, but most of the guys thought one cheat day a week wouldn't hurt anyone. Their performance on the field begged to differ.

Wyatt grabbed one of the few bottles of water and looked around. "Well, this is fun."

"I guess there are worse ways to spend a Saturday night." Tyrone stole a can of something without caffeine and popped the tab. "So what was it like playing for the Vigilantes?"

"Awesome. They were my dream team, you know?"

"Yeah. We're all wondering how you ended up with the Coyotes."

It wasn't like Wyatt had been immune to the whispers about his trade, but he flinched at the blatant question in Tyrone's eyes. "I guess I was ready for a change of scenery."

A group of laughing women spilled into the kitchen, empty beer cans in their hands. Wyatt leaned against the counter and took a sip of his water as the women reached for more alcohol. Man, their laughter was shrill. They pushed their way back out of the room, squeezing past someone new. A tall man stood in the doorway, a long dirty blond ponytail hanging down his back.

Drew.

Heat raced up Wyatt's spine and he clutched the water bottle in one fist, feeling the plastic give underneath his strength.

Drew zeroed in on Wyatt and lumbered across the kitchen, a grim smile on his face. "Thought I might run into you here."

How had he known about the party? Wyatt set his water bottle on the counter and folded his arms, refusing to let his former quarterback intimidate him. "What are you doing here?"

"Schroeder's an old friend."

Wyatt wasn't surprised. The two were practically carbon copies of each other.

Drew took a step closer. Behind him, Wyatt felt Tyrone step closer as well.

"I came here to warn you to stay away from Tamera," Drew said. His tone was menacing, his eyes narrowed into slits.

Her name had the hair on Wyatt's neck standing on end. He leaned forward, not caring that Drew had two inches and fifty pounds on him. "Maybe you haven't noticed, but Tamera's an adult capable of making her own decisions."

"Not this one."

Anger flared in Wyatt's chest and he fought to hold it back. This man had stolen his girlfriend, lied about what happened on the field, and then gotten Wyatt traded to a B-list team. "Don't tell me how to live my life, man."

Drew shoved Wyatt in the chest. He stumbled backward, caught off guard by the physical contact. In another moment he was in control again and shot forward. He'd been dreaming about hitting Drew for months, and now he'd finally get the chance.

Tyrone jumped between them, holding his arms out to keep them apart. "Whoa, whoa, whoa. Let's all take about five giant steps back and cool off a bit."

Wyatt's chest heaved, but he refused to back down. He glared at Drew, hate flowing through him.

"We don't want any trouble, Dempsey, okay?" Tyrone said. "We're just here to have a good time."

Maybe that worked for Tyrone, but Wyatt was done being pushed around. He stabbed a finger in Drew's direction. "What lies did you tell her?"

A slow grin spread across Drew's face. "I didn't tell her anything that wasn't true—just spun the story in my favor."

"She deserves to know the truth."

"She deserves the best."

Wyatt laughed. "Fine. Tell her whatever you want. Tamera's smart enough to see through your crap. She's way too smart to go for a cretin like you."

Drew held out his arms, taking a step back. "Looks like she already has, bro. You've lost. When are you going to realize that and stop trying to play a game you're not even second string in?"

Wyatt lunged at Drew, but Tyrone shoved him back.

"Cool off, bro. Don't give him what he wants," Tyrone said.

Wyatt shuddered, then nodded and took a step back. "Let's get out of here."

Tyrone nodded and they brushed past Drew. It took a lot of effort not to shove him, but Wyatt held back. Barely.

"She's mine, James," Drew called after him.

Wyatt froze, but Tyrone rested a heavy arm around his shoulders and propelled him forward. "Not worth it, man."

Not worth it. Wyatt let out a curse, but let Tyrone lead him from the house. They pushed past teammates and cheerleaders who barely seemed to notice their departure. Schroeder certainly wouldn't realize they'd left, and besides, they'd stuck around long enough to satisfy him even if he did.

"I hate that guy," Wyatt said as he dropped heavily into the passenger seat of Tyrone's Maserati.

"He's a total tool," Tyrone agreed as he started the car. "What was that all about, anyway?"

"Drew and I didn't exactly get along in San Antonio."

"Yeah, I caught that. What happened?"

Wyatt looked out the window as dark palm trees passed by in a blur. "It's a long story." One he needed to tell Tamera, and soon.

Chapter Sixteen

W hat a weekend. Tamera rolled over in bed with a groan. Had it really only been two days ago when her almost-kiss with Wyatt had been interrupted by the truth-bombs Drew dropped?

On Friday night, Drew's attempts to distract her had ended with one too many margaritas and fending off Drew's tipsy advances. He hadn't done more than make suggestive comments and once almost kiss her, but it had been enough for her to ignore him yesterday over claims she needed to work. It had been a flat-out lie. She hadn't shown any houses, or even cracked open the lid of her laptop. Instead she'd spent the day watching police procedurals and wondering what Wyatt would think of them.

"How do I always get into these messes?" she asked her ceiling.

With the heat of the moment past, Tamera tried to look at things objectively. She knew Wyatt—maybe not well, but she felt like he'd been genuine during their time together. And the Wyatt she knew wasn't a vengeful lover bent on total destruction. Maybe Drew had misinterpreted the situation. He was so closely involved—it would be easy to unintentionally exaggerate, given the men's history together.

She needed to talk to Wyatt. And she would text him today, once she worked up the courage. In the meantime, social media seemed like a great distraction.

Five minutes into scrolling through her feed, she saw a picture of Wyatt and Drew.

"Shut the front door," Tamera yelled. She sat up in bed, staring at the image. There was no mistaking the two men. Drew's ponytail hung down his back, his massive arms practically hulking out of his gray T-shirt. Wyatt stood toe-to-toe with Drew, his arms pushing against Drew's shoulders as though forcing the man to take a step back. Wyatt's jaw was clenched, his face all hard lines.

Was it an old photo? Tamera quickly scrolled up. She wasn't friends with whoever had posted the image, but Drew had been tagged. The photo had been captioned with one simple line—*Seems like not everyone's enjoying the party tonight.* It had only been posted last night, but where would both Drew and Wyatt have been?

Tamera zoomed in on the photo and squinted. It looked like they stood in a kitchen, but not one she recognized. The lighting was poor, and she could just make out dark granite countertops and slate gray Shaker cabinets. It would almost make sense if they had run into each other at a restaurant. But someone's house?

Drew had texted last night, asking Tamera to go with him to a party. She'd insisted she had a headache and begged off. At the time, she hadn't found it odd that Drew had found a party to attend. He was a social guy who knew a lot of people. But it must've been a party thrown by someone in the football world for Wyatt to also be there. Maybe Drew was a party animal, but Wyatt was more the quiet-evening-at-home type. And if it had been a football party, Drew would've at least suspected Wyatt might attend. But then why would Drew invite Tamera to the party? It didn't make sense.

She scrolled through the comments, her stomach doing cartwheels as she read each one. The photo was public, which meant the comments were already closing in on a thousand. Speculations ran rampant over what the argument had been about, and whether or not it factored into Wyatt's trade to L.A. If Drew was telling the truth, it most definitely had.

Her phone buzzed and she opened it to find a text from Wyatt. **Can we get together sometime soon? I'd love to talk.**

She ran her thumb over the edge of her phone, biting her bottom lip. Drew had told her to stay away. After his story, she understood why he was making the suggestion. But part of her couldn't quite believe that Wyatt would behave that way.

Drew told me a lot of things, Tamera typed back slowly.

I'm sure he did. But there are two sides to every story. Don't I get a chance to tell you mine?

She flopped back against her pillows, mind whirling as her emotions battled for dominance. **You can come over tonight,** she finally texted back.

Eight o'clock? I've got practice until then.

Okay.

She tapped her phone against one leg, then got out of bed with a groan. Eight o'clock was a long ways away, and she had house showings lined up for clients and lines to rehearse. Time to forget about Wyatt.

Yeah, right. Like that was even a possibility.

The day dragged by. Tamera showed small homes desperately in need of face lifts to clients on a shoestring budget all morning. That afternoon, she tried to avoid thinking about Wyatt while she prepared for her audition tomorrow. Then, because she was out of groceries, she headed to the store for some quick shopping.

That proved to be a bad idea. She got stuck in a line manned by a cashier-in-training. Her plan to make up time by speeding home was dashed by an accident that had traffic slowed to a crawl. By the time she pulled into the parking lot, Wyatt's truck was already in a visitor spot.

She loaded down her arms with bags of groceries and raced up the steps. She could see Wyatt's large figure from down the hallway and her palms grew sweaty, making the plastic bags slip in her hands.

"Sorry," she wheezed, out of breath. "Traffic."

He gave her a tentative smile that seemed to ask "are we okay?"

She wasn't sure. But she desperately wanted him to give an explanation that made Drew's claims seem like an overreaction. And that freaked her out.

"Here, let me help you." Wyatt reached for her bags, his warm hands brushing against hers and sending shock waves up her arms.

"Thanks." She fumbled for her keys, head swimming with conflicting emotions.

Wyatt set the bags on her kitchen counter, lifting the heavy sacks that had her out of breath like they weighed nothing. She folded her arms, her heart doing funny things at the sight of him in her kitchen. Last time he'd been here, they'd held each other close while entire books were written in the silence between them.

"How about I pull stuff out of the bags and you put it away?" Wyatt asked. "I'm not sure where things go, and I know from Natalie not to mess with a woman's kitchen."

Against Tamera's will, a smile twitched at her lips. She would love to meet the sister he spoke so fondly of. "You don't have to help."

"I know, but I want to."

"Okay then. Thanks."

She took her place beside him, the tension in the room weighing on her like a physical presence. Neither of them spoke as Wyatt pulled containers out of bags and Tamera placed things in the pantry or fridge. He worked efficiently, grouping like items together like he'd done this a dozen times before.

While on *Eye in the Sky*, contestants had been responsible for the day-to-day stuff. The show provided food, but it was up to the house guests to prepare meals, wash dishes, and clean the residence. She couldn't remember Drew pitching in even once. Just a few days ago, in fact, Drew had sat at the counter and watched while she cleaned up the remnants of dinner with Wyatt before they went out for the night. Caleb had never been an especially helpful boyfriend, either, often teasing her about "women's work" as an excuse for not doing whatever small task she'd asked of him. But Wyatt was working alongside her, helping. A guy who did that couldn't be the kind of guy Drew had painted.

Tamera placed the last can on the pantry shelf, then took her time wadding up the plastic bags and stowing them in the recycle bin underneath the kitchen sink. She wasn't sure how to broach this conversation, or what to say. Falling for Wyatt had never been part of the plan. She didn't know who or what to believe. Her track record wasn't exactly stellar when it came to trusting men.

Wyatt leaned against the counter and folded his arms, his brown eyes gazing at her steadily. She swallowed hard. Those eyes were so full of compassion and worry. Already she could feel herself being sucked in again.

"Are we going to talk about it?" he asked quietly.

Tamera lifted a shoulder in a shrug. "Are we?"

"I think we should." He looked away, then cleared his throat as though fighting back emotion. "I want you to know the truth."

His voice was a soft caress and she barely held back a shiver. She rubbed her hands up and down her arms and pushed past Wyatt. "We might as well sit down so we're comfortable." She had a feeling this might take a while.

Tamera nestled into one corner of the couch and expelled a breath when Wyatt took the chair across from her instead of the opposite end of the couch. His presence clouded her judgment and right now she needed a clear head. She tucked her feet underneath her and hugged a pillow to her chest, overcome by deja vu. Hadn't she just done this with Drew a couple of days ago? She suddenly felt very unsure and self-conscious.

Wyatt's muscled body dwarfed her gray armchair, but somehow he still managed to look lost and insecure. He rested his elbows on his knees and clasped his hands together, looking up at her from beneath hooded lids. "I guess Drew told you about what happened in San Antonio."

Tamera gave a small nod, playing with the edge of the pillow. She was still struggling to process that conversation.

"What did he say?"

So much, and separating fact from fiction was proving almost impossible. If she told him what Drew had said, Wyatt might alter his narrative to tell the story he wanted her to believe instead of the one that was true. She desperately wanted the truth. And she wanted it to paint Wyatt in a positive light.

"I'd like to hear your side of the story first," Tamera said.

Wyatt gave a short nod. "That's fair. I guess it all started with my first day on the Vigilantes, since that's where Drew and I met. We didn't really interact much in San Antonio—not initially, at least."

She kept her face impassive. At least his story was matching Drew's so far.

"We worked together in practice, but that was pretty much the only time we talked to each other."

"So you didn't get along from the beginning?"

"No, it wasn't that we didn't get along." Wyatt shifted in the chair, and her eyes followed his movements. "We just didn't talk. Our relationship wasn't good or bad, because it didn't exist. We were coworkers who nodded to each other in the locker room and worked together on the field, but that was it. Drew had been on the team a season longer than me and already had a bit of a reputation. I figured the wisest course of action was to steer clear of him as much as possible."

"What kind of reputation?" Tamera cut in.

Wyatt shrugged. "Just that he wasn't someone you wanted to cross."

Diary room interviews and things she'd seen on *Eye in the Sky* pushed forward in a surge of memories, all of them clamoring for attention. Drew had presented a congenial face to the house guests, flirting with the women and palling around with the guys, all while being ruthless behind closed doors.

It was a game, she reminded herself. Just because he'd played a cutthroat game on the show didn't mean that was who he really was.

How well did she really know Drew? They'd texted since leaving the house and seen each other a few times, mostly for interviews. But was that the same thing as knowing someone?

"I tried to stay out of his way as much as possible, because I wasn't interested in trouble," Wyatt continued. "I finally had my dream, you know? I've wanted to play for the Vigilantes since I was six years old. I used to watch their games with my dad and we'd talk about the day when I'd finally be a part of the team. They were so proud when I was picked in the draft."

His words did funny things to Tamera's emotions and she swallowed hard. Now was not the time to get all teary-eyed at the thought of Wyatt as a little boy with big ambitions and dreams.

"Then I met Becky."

"Your girlfriend?" Tamera clarified.

"Ex-girlfriend. But yeah." Wyatt blew out a deep breath. "Looking back, I can see that there were red flags from the beginning. But I was so enamored. Becky was beautiful and funny—the type of girl all the guys were jealous of. She was the prom queen and head cheerleader all rolled into one. I couldn't believe she was paying attention to me."

"I can believe it," Tamera said softly.

Wyatt's lips turned up in the barest hint of a smile. "Well, it was too good to be true. We'd been dating about six months when I found her in the locker room with Drew. The two of them were attached to each other like holiday window clings or something."

Again, that was pretty much the same story that Drew had told her. Tamera's hands tightened around the throw pillow. Maybe neither Drew or Wyatt were wrong. Maybe they just had different perspectives on the same crummy situation.

"I was completely stunned to find them together."

"You didn't suspect she was cheating?" Tamera asked quietly.

Wyatt shook his head. "No. I was totally blindsided. When I found them, Becky started crying and said she had made a mistake. But Drew just stood there, smirking. He said if I wasn't man enough to keep my woman occupied, then I shouldn't blame her when she went looking elsewhere."

Pinpricks of pain stabbed behind Tamera's eyes, and she put her hands to her temples and began to massage. This part of the story sounded unlike the Drew she knew, and yet at the same time she could totally picture the Drew from *Eye in the Sky* pulling something like that. Who was the real man? "That's not quite how Drew told the story."

Wyatt looked away, running one thumb over the other. "Yeah, well, the truth isn't very flattering."

"So what happened after that?"

"I told Becky we were over. She kept crying and insisting I give her another chance, but I was done at that point. That's when things started getting really tense."

Tamera pictured the scene, Wyatt and Drew caught in the middle of an overly emotional female who clearly made bad decisions.

"I knew Drew and Becky were dating, but she kept showing up at my house. She was sending me emails, spamming me with texts, leaving me dozens of voice mails ... you name it. She kept begging for me to take her back. When I'd ask if she was still with Drew, she'd get hysterical or defensive and refuse to answer the question. I think he knew she was still contacting me and the situation bled over into practice. Drew got really aggressive. He was constantly getting after me for not protecting him well enough, even when I was doing my best. The never-ending criticism in front of everyone on the team shot my confidence. Becky's continuous emotional attacks were getting to me, too. I started having a hard time focusing in practice and Coach took notice. That's when Drew got hurt."

Tamera pulled the pillow tighter against her churning stomach. Drew's hadn't talked much about his injury while on *Eye in the Sky*, but she'd noticed how he'd roll his shoulder like it hurt after a competition. The way he favored that side. He'd mentioned he'd probably spend most of the upcoming season on the bench.

"I won't lie and say the injury wasn't partially my fault," Wyatt said. His eyes were pained, his lips pulled down in a frown. "If I'd done my job right, Drew wouldn't have gotten sacked. But I didn't make a deliberate choice to let him get hurt. One of the other team's players distracted me, and by the time I realized it was a decoy, I was too late. They took Drew down hard. Ended up with a penalty."

Tamera had watched the game where Drew was injured and Wyatt's explanation made sense. The refs and commentators had all assumed what Wyatt had just told Tamera—that he'd fallen for a decoy and Drew got hurt as a result of a bad game decision. But what if Drew was right and Wyatt had done it deliberately?

She closed her eyes and forced herself to breathe deeply. Someone she cared about was lying, and it made her want to throw up.

Maybe no one was lying. The mind was a powerful tool. It could have tricked one or both men into believing things that weren't necessarily true.

"Do you regret it?" Tamera whispered.

"Drew getting hurt?"

She nodded.

Slowly, Wyatt shook his head. "I'd be lying if I didn't say that my first reaction was he got what he deserved. It'd been about a month since I found him with Becky, and Drew had made my life miserable. It felt like karma's way of getting him back. But when the team doctor told us how bad it was, I felt awful. I didn't just hurt Drew, I hurt the entire team. But these kinds of things happen on the field. I didn't think much of it until Coach called me into his office and said Drew was claiming I'd let him get hurt deliberately."

Tamera stayed quiet, trying to read Wyatt's body language. His shoulders were hunched, his muscles tense and eyes large. He reached forward, grasping one of her hands between both of his. Warmth skittered up her arm and she hated her heart for pounding at his touch.

"I told Coach it wasn't true. And it's not, Tamera. I swear to you, I didn't choose to let Drew get hurt. It was an accident. Football's a rough game. Sometimes the quarterback gets injured."

She nodded, but didn't speak.

"That's when Drew brought out the video footage. We watched it over and over in Coach's office, Drew claiming I let him get injured and me claiming it was an accident. It took a few weeks, but eventually Coach sided with Drew. I never connected with Coach, and he and Drew were tight. In the end, they gave me a choice—I could agree to a trade, or they'd go to the press with their findings."

The words washed over her and she tried to process what she'd just heard. Drew had helped the coach force Wyatt's trade? Her first instinct was to deny he'd ever do something like that. But similar moves on *Eye in the Sky* told a different story.

"And here we are." Wyatt let out a deep sigh. "I knew there was no point in fighting to stay if the Vigilantes wanted me gone. Distance from Becky hasn't been the worst thing to come of the move. I think I've finally convinced her we're over and to move on. She hasn't contacted me since I got to California."

"I ... I don't know what to say," Tamera said finally.

Wyatt took her hands gently in his. "I know you have no reason to trust me. We barely know each other. But I'm telling you the truth, Tamera."

She pulled her hand from Wyatt's and stood. "I want to believe you. But if you're telling the truth, that means Drew's lying to me."

Wyatt rose as well. "I can't pretend to have a high opinion of Drew when I don't. But I'm not asking you to choose between us. All I'm asking is for you to give me a chance to prove to you the kind of guy I am."

She was melting, her entire body involuntarily leaning toward his. Longing for his arms to reach out and wrap her close. As though sensing her emotions, Wyatt's hand gently brushed her cheek, tucking a lock of hair behind her ear.

"I want to believe you," she whispered. "But I'm a notoriously bad judge of character when it comes to guys. You remember Caleb, right? My ex-boyfriend that cheated on me with my sister?"

"I can sit here and tell you all day that I'm not like that, but I know words are cheap and don't mean much without actions behind them." His lips pulled up in a pained smile. "I hate that he hurt you so much."

Her eyes filled with tears, and she blinked and took a step back. "After the wedding, I swore off men forever, you know."

A warm chuckle filled the room, and she wanted to place her hands on his chest to feel the vibrations. "I swore off women, too. My relationship with Becky totally blew up in my face."

She peeked up at him, her eyes searching his. Wyatt's brown eyes were all melting chocolate, turning her insides to goo. "Then what are we doing here?"

"I don't know." He held up his hands in a helpless shrug. "But I sure would like to see where it goes. Let me prove to you the kind of man I am. Can you trust me that much?"

She closed her eyes, fear nearly paralyzing her vocal cords. But a tiny seed of hope had her nodding. "Okay."

His hand cupped her cheek and she leaned into it. Her legs trembled with the magnitude of that one little word which promised a commitment she'd sworn she'd never give again.

"Does that mean you'll still go to Universal Studios with me?" Wyatt asked, his tone lighter than it had been all day.

Tamera laughed, tension oozing out of her as she let her shoulders relax. "Absolutely. I think it's high time I visit there."

"Good." Wyatt's breath wafted over here and she swayed toward him. "Can I get a hug?"

She didn't answer, just leaned into him and wrapped her arms around his waist. Her fingers barely met on the other side, but she buried her head in his chest and relished the feel of his strong arms around her. One of his large hands ran through her short hair, and she wanted to stay in that moment forever.

She'd taken a leap with Wyatt. Hopefully she didn't find herself bloodied and broken on the other side of the mountain.

Chapter Seventeen

W yatt closed his laptop, satisfaction rolling through him. Another script finished. That was his fifth one, although the first three had been before his pro football days. He leaned back in the uncomfortable hotel chair and stretched, groaning as his back cracked satisfyingly. His eyes ached from the dim lighting in his room, but that was okay. The next script he started would be in his new home office.

While he wrote the final scenes, he couldn't help but picture Tamera playing the part of his strong yet vulnerable heroine. Since their conversation three days ago, they'd been cautiously texting each other, mostly about the house. Today they'd meet with the inspector and if all went as planned he'd close on the house next week. But occasionally Tamera would slip something more personal into her texts. An offhanded mention that Drew was back in Texas. Disappointment over an audition she blew. Questions about his day. She hadn't completely shut him out, and that gave Wyatt hope.

The bright California sunshine, fresh air, and green grass of the football stadium were a welcome change from the stuffy hotel room that was starting to feel claustrophobic. Wyatt pushed himself hard in practice and was pleasantly surprised at how well it went. He hadn't thought it possible, but the team had made some real strides in the month since he'd been traded. Maybe McKinley was right, and Wyatt still had a chance at a championship before retirement. For the first time since Becky's betrayal, he let himself imagine what winning that game would feel like. The heart-pumping adrenaline. Sweat dripping down his back as he fought to protect the quarterback. Tamera cheering him on from the stands.

"Hellooooo. Earth to Wyatt." Tyrone waved a hand in front of his face and Wyatt snapped back to the present.

"Sorry." He set his deodorant back in the locker and pulled on a soft T-shirt. He had another commercial shoot in a few minutes and knew wardrobe would have their own ideas about what he should wear.

"You were on Planet Hot Realtor, weren't you?"

Wyatt couldn't stop the smile that spread across his lips. "I'd better get out to the field. Doing another commercial shoot today."

"Okay, okay. Don't tell me."

"See you tomorrow." Wyatt grinned and shut his locker door. Tyrone shook his head in exasperation and waved Wyatt off.

Outside, the field had already been transformed for the shoot. Wyatt was whisked away to wardrobe, then hair and makeup. He glanced at his watch. About four hours until he'd meet Tamera for the inspection. She had house showings before, so they'd agreed to just meet at the house.

He grabbed his phone off the small table cluttered with makeup brushes while two women fluttered around him.

"Hold still, sweetie," the first said. She had to be at least sixty, with the gravelly voice of a chain-smoker.

"Sorry," Wyatt mumbled. He stared at Tamera's number, then quickly sent a text before he could talk himself out of it. **Wish me luck.**

The ding of her response had Wyatt's breath quickening. **Good luck! Um, why am I wishing you luck?**

Another commercial shoot. He inserted a wild-eyed emoticon. **If we don't get a decent take or two, I may be responsible for one very frazzled producer switching careers.**

I'm sure it's not that bad.

You saw my fake smile, right?

Oh, is that what you were doing? I thought you were in pain.

Wyatt laughed out loud, earning a glare from Chain-Smoker.

Another text appeared from Tamera. **I never really got around to giving you tips, did I?**

In an instant, Wyatt was back in Tamera's living room, her soft hands pressed against his chest while his tangled in her hair. **I guess we both were a little distracted. ;)**

As soon as Wyatt sent the text, he second-guessed himself. The winky face had totally been overkill. He wasn't even sure if they were in a place where flirting was allowed.

The minutes ticked by and Wyatt grew more and more nervous. That winky face had definitely gone too far. He had to stop overplaying his hand with Tamera. She needed slow and steady. He was determined to give her that.

Chain-Smoker and her assistant finished with Wyatt, and he headed onto the field, the familiar nausea overtaking him.

"Ready for today?" the producer asked with a tight smile.

"I'm going to try my best," Wyatt said.

"Good."

Wyatt pulled his phone out of one pocket and was just about to set it on his chair when the screen lit up with a text.

Well, try and stay focused today, hot stuff. Don't miss the home inspection or else. ;)

Maybe he hadn't screwed up as badly as he feared. *Hot stuff.* He felt his confidence shoot up a notch at the flirtatious comment.

"Wyatt?" the producer said.

"Sorry." Wyatt dropped the phone and headed to his mark. Someone handed him the football and the director took his place.

"Action," the director called.

Wyatt took a step forward, determination filling him. No way was he missing a chance to see Tamera. He wasn't about to let this shoot run long.

They flew through the shots, doing fewer takes than ever before. Wyatt held on to his confidence with an iron fist, worried that one false move would send him back to becoming a bumbling idiot in front of the camera. He knew he wasn't great—nothing like Tamera had been on *Eye in the Sky*—but for the first time, he thought maybe he didn't suck, either.

"That's a wrap," the director called.

Wyatt's shoulder slumped and for the first time he became aware of how much they ached. How tense had he been? He handed over the football, and the director crossed to him.

"Great job today," he said. "You've really improved. What changed this time?"

"I'm not sure," Wyatt lied. He knew what the difference was. Tamera.

"Well, hold onto that for next time. Although I think we have enough footage for what Mr. Ryder needs. With any luck, we won't need anymore takes." He held out a hand. "It was a pleasure working with you, Mr. James."

"You as well," Wyatt lied. He hoped to never be in front of a camera again. Writing scripts was much more his style. But he had done it, and that wasn't a small accomplishment.

Wyatt quickly changed clothes, then reclaimed his phone and checked it for notifications. A text icon flashed on the screen and he quickly swiped it open. Hopefully Tamera hadn't been delayed at one of her showings.

But it wasn't Tamera who had texted him. His blood ran cold as he read the name.

Becky.

Pinpricks of ice stabbed at his heart. She hadn't contacted him in probably five or six weeks. What could she possibly want?

His eyes slid from the name to the message. **Can we talk? There's something I need to tell you.**

He shoved his phone in his pocket and headed to his truck, not answering Becky's text. There was nothing she could say that he wanted to hear. They'd only dated six months and Wyatt took their relationship at a glacial pace, much to Becky's frustration. He'd barely mustered up the courage to really kiss her by the time they broke up.

More head games. That's all the text was about. But he was done letting her mess with his mind.

Wyatt drove to the house—*his house*, he reminded himself, at least soon—and tried not to think about Becky. The last few weeks of silence had been so nice that he'd almost forgotten how horrible the barrage of texts and phone calls had been.

The home was as inviting as ever. Tingles of anticipation raced up Wyatt's spine as it came into view. He couldn't wait to pull his furniture out of storage and finally settle into life in California. It would be so nice to get a drink of water without walking down two flights of stairs for ice. To fall asleep on his own mattress. He missed his ergonomic keyboard and worn office chair.

Tamera's red convertible was nowhere to be seen. Wyatt rolled down his window and turned off the truck so it wouldn't idle. The warm sun beat down on his arm, and he leaned his head back against the headrest and sighed. At least the sun had the same soothing properties here as in Texas.

A low purr had him sitting up straight. Tamera's cherry red convertible pulled up behind his truck, the top down and radio playing a pop song.

Wyatt got out of the car and leaned against his door. Tamera looked breathtaking in her sleeveless blouse, white capris, and strappy sandals. He fought the urge to pull her into his arms and instead shoved his hands in his pockets. Man, he loved how she looked in sunglasses.

"Hey." Tamera perched the shades on top of her windblown hair and gave him a tentative smile.

He returned it with one of his own. "Hey. How'd the audition go?"

"Not bad. But that's what I thought last time and someone else got the part."

He nudged her shoulder with his own as they walked toward the front door. "You'll get there eventually."

"How did the commercial shoot turn out?"

"Shockingly enough, not horrible. The director seemed happy at least."

"That's progress." She unlocked the door and stepped inside. "The inspector should be here any minute. He texted to let me know he's running a little behind."

"I'm not in any hurry." Wyatt glanced at the entryway, taking in the house with new eyes. It was the first he'd seen it since deciding to make the purchase. He surveyed the room, imagining where he'd put his furniture. What things he'd have updated or changed.

"Still glad you're buying it?" Tamera asked.

He nodded, unable to stop smiling. "Yeah. I am."

"It's got good bones."

A knock sounded at the door and Tamera opened it to reveal a short, stooped man with wispy gray hair.

For the next two hours, the inspector went over every inch of the house with a fine-toothed comb. Tamera lagged behind Wyatt, letting him take the lead, but asked pertinent questions he'd never have thought of. With each room they went through, Wyatt's excitement grew. Natalie would love this place. He couldn't wait for her to visit with their parents next month.

The inspector snapped shut his clipboard, and Tamera and Wyatt walked him toward the front door. "I'll have my official report to you by tomorrow night," the inspector said. "But overall, I think it's a solid purchase. I didn't see any major red flags raised."

"That's what we like to hear," Tamera said cheerfully.

They said their goodbyes and Tamera shut the door behind the stooped man. With no furniture to cushion it, the sound echoed off the walls. Wyatt was acutely aware that they were once again alone.

"Anything else you want to look at before we leave?" Tamera asked.

"I guess not." Wyatt ran a hand over his head. "It'll be nice to finally move in and get settled."

"I can't imagine staying in a hotel for so long. You must be so sick of spending time there." She nudged his arm with her own. "Want to go to a movie tonight? That new detective film just released."

Wyatt fought to keep his jaw from dropping. He shoved his hands in his pockets and grinned. "Are you asking me out?"

Her lips pursed together and her eyes turned serious. "Call it a peace offering."

His hands itched to brush her hair behind one ear. Warmth was thawing his heart and he wanted to shout his thanks to the heavens. But instead, he just nodded, trying to play it cool. "Okay then. I accept."

Chapter Eighteen

Tamera hummed as she finished up her makeup, feeling her stomach twist and roll as butterflies dive-bombed her innards. Wyatt would be here soon to pick her up. She didn't know what she was more excited for—a date with Wyatt, or having that date at Universal Studios.

Going to the movies with him had been nearly perfect. They'd both stayed completely silent during the film, but it hadn't been awkward at all. Instead, Tamera had enjoyed seeing a movie with someone who appreciated the need for complete and total focus on the story. After the movie was over, they'd wandered the mall where the theater was located and spent nearly two hours dissecting everything from the plot to the script to the acting.

She was falling for Wyatt. Whether she wanted to admit it or not, that was the truth. Drew's warnings were holding less and less weight, especially considering he seemed to be pushing for something more lately—something she definitely wasn't interested in.

Tamera put away her lip gloss and fluffed her hair, then tugged at the hem of her shirt. She'd opted for a sheer polka dot blouse buttoned over a teal tank top, paired with her favorite pair of jean shorts and sandals that were cute but also comfortable. Who knew what cameras might point her way today? She'd be in the park with Wyatt James which was definitely a Kodak moment. Her agent would flip if she was photographed looking less than perfect.

A knock came at the front door and her heart started hammering in her chest. She pressed a hand flat over her stomach and took a deep breath. Today would be significant. A point from which she could never return. She could feel it in her bones.

She grabbed the small messenger purse from off the kitchen counter and opened the door. Her breath caught in her throat at the sight of Wyatt. He wore his Los Angeles Coyotes jersey, the dark blue fabric with gold accents bringing out the color of his eyes. Denim shorts hung loosely on his hips and a pair of sunglasses was tucked in the collar of his shirt.

"Wow," Tamera said. She stepped outside and locked her condo door. "I've never seen you in a jersey before."

Wyatt reached up and scratched the back of his head, looking embarrassed. "The colors still feel weird to me. Every time I slip into my uniform, I feel like something's wrong."

"Trust me, there is nothing wrong with how you look."

His chuckled and the warm sound sent shivers across her spine. "I could say the same for you. You look beautiful, as always."

She blushed and ducked her head. "Thank you."

They walked side by side to his car. She couldn't remember the last time she'd felt this safe and protected. Wyatt towered over her— completely dominated in size. But she knew he'd never do anything to hurt her. Instead, he held her door open like a perfect gentleman. Tamera stared up at the car seat, which was nearly as high as her shoulders. The lift on Wyatt's truck was insane.

"Let me help you," Wyatt said, his low voice sending shivers over her entire body. Then his hands were at her waist, feather-light as he lifted her into the cab of his truck like she didn't weigh a thing.

Tamera settled into the seat, running a hand over the dark gray fabric. Wyatt shut his door and the engine roared to life.

"Let's hope traffic isn't too bad," he said, putting the truck in gear.

Tamera laughed. "You know we're in California, right? Bad traffic is inevitable here, especially around Hollywood. That place is always crowded."

"Then I'll be doubly grateful to have you here to keep me company."

Her entire heart warmed. Tamera felt like she could float right out of his window on a cloud of contentment.

Traffic was atrocious, in typical L.A. fashion, but Tamera didn't mind crawling down the freeway at ten miles an hour when she had Wyatt sitting next to her, providing conversation.

"You can't seriously tell me you enjoyed that film," Tamera said. Her legs were stretched out underneath the dashboard, feet crossed at the ankle, more relaxed than she'd been in months.

Wyatt shot her a sideways look, one eyebrow raised. "You didn't?"

"Uh, no!" She held up two fingers on both hands and crossed them in a hashtag sign. "Hashtag box office flop."

"It only flopped because the acting was so awful."

Tamera rolled her eyes. "Uh, the acting is kind of the point of a movie."

"No," he shot back. "Without a fantastic script, there wouldn't be a movie to act badly in."

When was the last time she'd bantered with a guy and enjoyed it? She wracked her brain, but honestly couldn't remember. She and Drew had spent hours talking while on *Eye in the Sky*, but it had almost always been about the game and how they could win.

"Excellent actors can make up for a crappy script, but crappy actors can tank a good script," Tamera said. "Therefore, the acting is the most important element of a film."

Wyatt laughed, stretching his fingers on the steering wheel. Her eyes followed his strong hands as they flexed and straightened, mesmerized by the sinews and sun-bronzed skin. "Maybe you have a point."

"I'd love to read one of your scripts sometime." Tamera wanted a glimpse into Wyatt's mind. To see what kinds of stories he wrote, worlds he imagined, and characters he created.

The tips of Wyatt's ears turned red and he cleared his throat. "They're probably not any good. Nothing like the parts you audition for."

"Sure. That hemorrhoids commercial was real comedic gold."

He snorted and she felt immense pride at making him laugh. "Don't mention that in your Oscars acceptance speech."

She placed a hand lightly on his arm and felt his muscles tense in response. "Seriously. I want to read one of your scripts. You don't give yourself enough credit—I'm sure they're great."

His eyes flicked to hers, then back to the road. "Maybe someday I'll let you read one."

Warmth filled her heart at that one word—*someday*. It opened up a world of possibilities she desperately wanted to explore. "Have you ever written any characters that I'd play well?"

"None of those characters would do you justice."

She blushed. "Don't you mean I wouldn't do justice to the character?"

"No, I definitely mean the characters are too bland for you." His eyes slid her way. "Maybe in my next script, I'll write the heroine with you in mind."

Was she drooling? Because seriously, Wyatt was f-i-n-e.

Tamera's phone buzzed, startling her. She fumbled to pull it from her purse. Had she ever forgotten about her phone before? Probably not. But something about Wyatt made her want to live completely in the moment.

She flicked open the screen and saw a text from Drew. **What are you doing tonight? Thought maybe you could catch a flight to San Antonio and we could hang.**

Um, was he freaking insane? She fought the urge to text him back *#inyourdreams*. Friends didn't hop planes to fly halfway across the country for a weekend. That was something couples did. And they would never be a couple. Drew was a great friend, but she wasn't interested in him romantically. She'd always thought his harmless flirtations were just that, but lately he was definitely acting like a man who wanted something more.

Wyatt glanced over at her phone, then back at the road. "Everything okay?"

"Oh. Yeah." She dropped her phone back in her purse, not sure if Drew was a subject she could bring up with Wyatt just yet. "I swear, I'm ready to chuck my phone in the Pacific. People I'm trying to ignore keep bugging me."

"That doesn't sound like fun."

"It's not." She ran a hand over the zipper on her purse. If she mentioned Drew's sudden interest, Wyatt would get defensive. The two had so much history. But having someone besides Drew to talk to about Caleb would be a relief. "It's my ex. The one who's now my brother-in-law?"

Wyatt nodded, motioning for her to go on.

"Well, he keeps texting me. From his honeymoon. Although I guess they're back in Texas by now." She rested an arm on the window, threading her fingers through her hair.

"Whoa."

"Yeah, I know. Katie keeps sending me pictures of the fabulous time she's having. Meanwhile, he offered me the role of mistress."

Wyatt's hands tightened on the steering wheel and his jaw clenched. "I will never understand men like that. He seriously propositioned you?"

"More or less." Tamera sighed. "I want to tell Katie about what Caleb did, but I'm not sure how. I told him to leave me alone, so I'm hoping it's just a one-time thing. I haven't heard from him again at least."

"That's a tough spot to be in."

Tough. Impossible. Awful. Take your pick, because none of those adjectives were wrong. Tamera turned in her seat, making the belt stretch taut over her shoulder, and gave Wyatt her full attention. "Has Becky ever done crazy things like this?"

He chuckled darkly, making the hairs on her arms stand on end. "Not quite that crazy. But yeah, she tried pretty hard to get me back while still dating..."

Drew. That single name hung between them, an elephant in the room they couldn't quite get past.

Wyatt cleared his throat. "Anyway, she sent me a text again just the other day."

"Seriously?" Tamera asked in surprise.

Wyatt nodded. "I haven't texted her back. I guess I'm hoping it's a one-time thing, too, and that she's not gearing up to ambush me again."

"We're quite the pair, aren't we?"

Wyatt reached across the console and squeezed her hand for the briefest of moments. His touch was so light, she almost wondered if she'd imagined it. "Everyone's got baggage."

Tamera didn't like the somber mood that had fallen over the cab. She pointed up ahead and purposefully made her voice light, eager to recapture the playfulness from earlier. "Hey, we can finally see the exit. We're almost there."

"Only took two hours," Wyatt joked.

He coasted off the exit, and Tamera felt her stomach tighten with excitement as they passed the sign for Universal Studios Hollywood. In the parking garage, an attendant motioned them to a preferred spot right outside the gate, which had been reserved for the team.

Tamera hopped out of the truck and stared up at the park in awe. She felt Wyatt step beside her and looked up into his face. His hands were shoved deep in his pockets, the baseball cap she'd grown used to seeing him wear in public gone. Today, he wasn't trying to hide.

"Should we go check it out?" Wyatt asked.

"Absolutely," Tamera breathed.

They quickly made their way through security, then Tamera grabbed Wyatt's hand and tugged him toward the red carpet. "Come on. We have to get our picture beneath the arch."

Wyatt laughed and followed her willingly toward the carpet. A photographer motioned for them to stand on the red carpet, beneath the white backdrop and park sign.

"Closer," the photographer said.

Tamera felt Wyatt's hand rest lightly on her waist. She leaned into him, heart pounding furiously as she smiled for the picture.

Wyatt took a step back and cleared his throat. "Ready to go inside?"

"I think I was born ready," Tamera teased.

He laughed and they made their way to the ticket carousel, then inside the park. Tamera put a hand to her chest, feeling tears prick unexpectedly at her eyes as she took in everything.

Wyatt's shoulder nudged hers gently. "You okay?"

She laughed. "I'm perfect. I just can't believe I'm finally here."

"Most of the day is ours. In about an hour, I've got to go to the gender reveal party Brooke and Luke are doing. It's a big deal I guess, and all the media will be there."

"Uh, yeah, a baby is a big deal."

"You know what I mean."

"I'm not surprised they're doing it with the team. They're America's favorite couple, and it's a good way to get positive PR for the Coyotes."

"I had no idea these kinds of parties were a thing until Luke told us about it and McKinley threatened us with ladder drills if we didn't show up. But it should be pretty easy." Wyatt pulled open his map and pointed to the Minions ride. "They're doing it here, since it's the most kid friendly area of the park. All we've got to do is stand there and smile."

"Sounds good," Tamera said. "What else is on the schedule?"

"I've got a Q&A scheduled at two o'clock, followed by a meet and greet. That'll take about two hours, probably—sorry about that. But otherwise, we can do whatever we want. Our instructions are to have a good time, wander around the park, and interact with fans."

"Hey, I'm just happy you chose to take me along for the ride." Tamera glanced up at Wyatt, hardly able to believe they were finally on a date. "What do you want to do?"

"Everything." Wyatt grinned and his entire face lit up like a kid's at Christmas. "I think I'm most excited for the studio tour, though."

"Me too," Tamera said.

"Good. Let's do that right after the gender reveal, then."

Tamera pointed in the direction of the Minions ride. "We probably have time to go on the ride before the party."

"Let's do it," Wyatt said.

The park was crowded, but their front-of-the-line passes significantly cut down the wait time. Wyatt waved to the excited kids waiting in line, and stopped for a few pictures and autographs before an employee finally ushered them onto the ride. Tamera's heart swelled as she watched Wyatt interact with the fans. He was so genuine and caring. It only made her fall for him harder.

By the time they stumbled out of the Minion ride, their eyes blinking rapidly to adjust to the sudden brightness after the 3D glasses, a small crowd had gathered around the platform erected outside the ride. Reporters milled around while cameramen wrestled with equipment. Tamera even recognized a few familiar faces from Toujour.

"Looks like it's nearly time." Wyatt pointed to the team, gathered near the front. "Stay close so I don't lose you in the crowd."

Tamera hovered behind Wyatt, allowing him to blaze a path through the people. Zoey, one of the matchmakers from Toujour, waved enthusiastically at Tamera from her spot near the front. A thin man with dark skin stood beside her, his posture stiff and face lined with stress. But then Zoey looked up at him and said something, and his entire face transformed into a look of utter love.

"That's Zoey and Mitch," Wyatt said, waving at the couple as well. "Mitch is Luke's personal assistant, and Zoey is Brooke's best friend. They got married not too long ago."

"Yeah, I recognize Zoey from Toujour," Tamera said.

"Right. I always forget you used to be a client."

Wyatt settled in at the back of the pack of teammates. Tamera stuck to his side, hardly believing she was surrounded by an entire football team.

"Wyatt, man." A man with dark skin and a shaved head held out a hand, and the two clapped each other on the backs in a man hug.

"Good to see you, Tyrone." Wyatt placed a hand gently on Tamera's back. "This is Tamera."

"Nice to meet you," Tyrone said, giving her a big smile. "I've heard a lot about you."

"Only good things, I hope," Tamera said as a thrill went through her. Wyatt had talked about her to his teammates. That had to mean something.

"Nothing but praise," Tyrone assured her.

Zoey made her way onto the stage, looking very old Hollywood in a red halter dress with white polka dots. "Hey, everyone," she said. "We're all so excited to find out what Brooke and Luke's bun in the oven is!"

Hoots filled the crowd from the direction of what Zoey assumed were Brooke and Luke's friends and family.

"Don't worry, we're not going to hold you in suspense for too long," Zoey said. "Pull out your cameras, everyone, and put your hands together for Brooke and Luke!"

Brooke and Luke walked onto the platform, practically glowing with happiness. Brooke wore a floral empire-waist garden dress, and Luke looked impeccable as always in a suit and tie. Hard to believe Tamera had once gone on a date with the man. She'd been so starstruck at the time. Little had she known that date would propel her into a world where she'd meet a lot more celebrities. Become friends with a few of them. Maybe even fall in love with a dashing football player who made her knees go weak.

"Thank you for coming," Brooke said into the microphone. She placed a hand on her stomach. "Luke and I couldn't be more excited to share this with everyone here today. We've waited for this moment for a long time."

Wyatt leaned down, his lips just brushing Tamera's ear. "They look happy, don't they?"

"The happiest," Tamera agreed.

He pointed to a couple standing near the front of the crowd. A pretty woman with dark blonde hair stood beside a man with a lanky figure. "That's Andi. She works for Footsteps for Change, the foundation we're doing this for. She helped arrange this whole thing."

"She dated Luke, too," Tamera said, suddenly recognizing the woman from the papers. They'd also been setup through Toujour and ended up going out for a month or two.

"Not anymore," Wyatt said. "She's engaged to that guy, Ben."

"They look happy, too," Tamera said.

Brooke had stopped talking, and she and Luke now stood beside a four-foot tall box striped pink and blue.

"Ready?" Luke asked.

Brooke nodded. "One ... two ... three!"

They lifted the lid of the box off together and dozens of pink balloons floated toward the sky. The crowd erupted in cheers, and Tamera laughed and clapped.

"It's a girl," Tamera said as Brooke and Luke hugged each other close.

Wyatt grinned. "Congrats to the new parents. Now let's get out of here. I'm dying to explore this place."

Chapter Nineteen

Tamera leaned into Wyatt, feeling a rush of delight as the tram drove silently past a hot set. The outdoor town square was mostly obscured by cameras and backdrops, but she could still make out a few boom mics and actors between all the other equipment.

An actual Hollywood movie was being filmed right before her eyes. Incredible.

The set disappeared from sight as the tram pulled up a hill, and then the voice of the tour guide crackled over the microphone. "Thanks for your cooperation back there, folks. Next up, we'll check out the set that's frequently used to film scenes set in Europe."

"This is so cool," Tamera breathed, glanced up at Wyatt. Sunglasses hid his eyes, but the air of mystery it lent to him was beyond attractive.

"What movie do you think they were filming?" Wyatt asked.

Tamera pursed her lips, thinking. "Hard to say. I know a sequel to the buddy cop movie that hit it big last year is underway."

"The wordplay in that movie was brilliant," Wyatt said. "I couldn't stop laughing."

"The wordplay was decent," Tamera countered, holding up a hand. "It was the actors who made it funny. Their delivery was perfect."

Wyatt stretched his arm around the back of her seat, his hand hovering mere inches from her shoulder. "I think we need to watch that movie again—this time together—to gather ammunition for our future arguments."

"Well, you do have a fantastic home theater that you'll need to christen."

"It's a date."

Her heart was melting into a puddle of goo and Tamera didn't even care.

The tram approached a body of water, with small beach-style cottages on the opposite shore.

"Here is where the Steven Spielberg classic *Jaws* was filmed," the tour guide said. "Don't worry, folks. No sharks here today. We've got some divers checking the waters, just to be safe. And ... oh dear."

Tamera laughed as she watched a single shark fin appear above the water, just behind the robotic diver.

"Sir, get out of the water," the tour guide said urgently. "Sir!"

Wyatt laughed, bringing a hand to his mouth and hollering, "Get out of the water."

The kids in the car behind them took up the call as the shark fin drew ever closer to the diver.

"Oh no," the tour guide said. "Kids, look away. I don't want you to —oh dear."

The diver disappeared beneath the surface in a sea of bubbles while the water became tinged with red.

"I'm sure he's fine," the tour guide said as the tram began moving again. "Probably just playing dead. There's nothing to worry abo—"

A shark leapt from the water, it's mouth opened wide, displaying rows of wicked-looking teeth. Tamera screamed and shrank into Wyatt, her heart pounding frantically in her chest.

Wyatt's arm wrapped around her, his breath hot on her ear as a low chuckle made his chest reverberate.

Tamera laughed, sagging against Wyatt in relief.

"I was not expecting that," she admitted.

"Me either." Wyatt brushed a strand of hair out of her face and tucked it behind her ear. "You're trembling."

"Yeah, well, I almost had a heart attack." She stared up into his deep brown eyes, her voice a lot breathier than she'd intended it to be.

His knuckles caressed her cheek. "Don't worry," he whispered, his eyes holding hers with a promise she desperately wanted to accept. "I'll protect you."

She rested one hand on his cheek. It was involuntary, like two magnets she couldn't pull apart. But Wyatt didn't flinch. Didn't pull away. "Are you sure you can handle me? I'm kind of a mess."

"I think I'm up to the challenge." His eyes flicked to her lips, then back to her eyes with a silent question.

Tamera didn't move her hand from his cheek. She barely remembered to breathe as his head descended toward hers.

"Ew!" one of the boys said from the row in front of them, his nose wrinkled in disgust. "Wyatt James has a girlfriend."

"Gross," the girl sitting next to him said with a giggle.

Tamera's face heated and she dropped her forehead to Wyatt's chest, her shoulder shaking with repressed laughter.

Wyatt brushed back her hair. She could feel him laughing as well, his strong muscles shaking against her body. "Sorry," he muttered. "I guess I forgot where we were for a moment."

"Yeah. Me too."

Tamera barely paid attention to the rest of the hour-long tour. She was all too aware of the strong man sitting beside her, his hand engulfing hers in its protective warmth.

At last the tram pulled back up to the ride entrance. Wyatt held out his hand, helping Tamera down before he was swarmed by eager kids begging for an autograph or picture. Tamera let the kids push their way in front of her and lingered at the back of the pack for a moment. Then she found a raised flowerbed shaded by a tree and sat on the ledge, watching from a distance.

Wyatt was incredible with the kids. With the younger ones, he crouched down so he was at their eye-level. With the older ones, he held out his hand for a fist bump and smiled for selfies. Everyone adored Wyatt and it was easy to see why. Tamera kind of adored him, too.

At last, the crowd dispersed and Wyatt made his way back to Tamera.

"Sorry about that," he said, his lips turned up in an apologetic smile.

Tamera rose and straightened her messenger purse strap. "Don't be. That's why you're here today. I enjoy watching you."

He fell into step beside her. "Well, I'm all yours until the next crowd descends. Where should we go next?"

Tamera shrugged, content just to walk beside Wyatt. "Where would Luke or your coach want you to be?"

Wyatt's hand bumped against hers again, making it hard for Tamera to think clearly. "I think Luke's probably too busy taking care of his pregnant wife to care what we do. And Coach would say to go wherever it's the most crowded right now so we can interact with the fans. That's going to be the rides, I think. Maybe later we can check out some of the shows."

"Sounds good," Tamera breathed.

Wyatt took a deep breath, then his fingers threaded tentatively through hers. "Is this okay?" he asked in a low, husky voice.

Tamera brushed a strand of hair behind one ear, unable to stop the grin splitting her face. "More than okay."

"Good."

Wyatt consulted his phone for ride wait times, never letting go of her hand, and determined that the Lower Lot was most crowded right now —probably because everyone wanted to fight the heat of the day by getting wet on the Jurassic Park ride. They rode the numerous escalators down to that end of the park, chatting with the fans in front of and behind them on the steps.

Once they reached the ground, Wyatt tugged Tamera toward the Jurassic Park ride. She thought he was going to get in line, but instead he pulled her into a secluded corridor.

Tamera looked up at the trees shading them on one side, and the stucco wall on the other. "What's back here?"

"A play area for toddlers," Wyatt said, consulting his phone before shoving it back in one pocket. "I figured it'd be pretty empty right now. I just need a minute."

Tamera rested a hand on his arm, instantly concerned. "Are you okay?"

"Yeah." He ran a hand over his head. "Crowds just drain me. I need a minute to decompress before I go back out there."

"Okay." Tamera leaned against the wall, watching as Wyatt did the same. His breaths were slow and even—no signs of panic or distress. "I've never seen this side of you before."

His mouth quirked up in a grin. "That's kind of the point. I hide when I need a second to recharge so the cameras don't realize what an introvert I am."

An introvert. It totally fit with what she'd seen of Wyatt so far. "Yeah, I've never had that problem."

Wyatt laughed, pushing off the wall to face her. He threaded his fingers through hers again. "Are you having a good time?"

"The best." Tamera pressed closer to the wall, her knees suddenly a little weak. Wyatt was so close—barely a foot separated them.

Wyatt seemed to sense her train of thought and he took a step closer. "What's been your favorite part of the day?"

"Uh, seeing the hot set," Tamera said. Her thoughts were scattering as her spine tingled, and she didn't even care.

Wyatt ran a hand through her hair and she shivered. "My favorite part was definitely when the shark scared you to death."

Tamera laughed, lightly punching him in the chest. "You would enjoy that part."

His hand captured hers and held it against his chest. She could feel the hard muscles beneath her palm. Found herself leaning into him without consciously telling her body to do so.

"I enjoyed how you scooted closer to me," he said, his voice husky.

"Yeah, well, you have a very protective presence," Tamera said, her voice much breathier than she meant it to be.

Wyatt's eyes flicked to her lips and his head lowered. Tamera raised up on tiptoes, threading her hands together behind the back of his neck and urging him the last few centimeters. She wanted this. Ached for it.

This time, no one interrupted. Wyatt's lips brushed against hers once, a feather-light kiss that had her insides trembling. Tamera let her fingers run over the short stubble of hair on his head, loving how soft it felt beneath her fingertips. Then they were kissing again, and this time, it most definitely wasn't soft or gentle. Tamera leaned against the wall for support, and then Wyatt's hands were at her waist, lifting her into his arms and drawing her closer. She let her feet leave the ground as his jaw worked against hers.

She'd never understood what people meant when they said they saw fireworks during a kiss. Now, she totally got it.

Wyatt groaned, tightening his hold as she opened her mouth, allowing him to deepen the kiss. This. This is what love was supposed to feel like. As Wyatt's lips expertly moved against hers, she knew it wasn't just his skill that had her seeing fireworks. It was a deeper, emotional connection. Something she'd never before experienced.

Wyatt set her back on the ground and rested his forehead against hers, breathing heavily. "We'd better get in line for Jurassic Park."

Tamera rested her hands on his chest, her own breathing none too steady. "Why?"

"Because I think we should be with other people right now."

Tamera grinned, a thrill of happiness surging through her. "Yeah. That's probably a good idea."

Wyatt's head dipped down, claiming her lips once more. Tamera was just starting to enjoy herself when he pulled and tugged her toward the crowd streaming by their little alcove. "Come on."

Tamera stumbled after Wyatt, her head lighter than she could ever remember it feeling. She brought her free hand to her cheek. It was impossible to stop grinning.

Wyatt James had kissed her. Wyatt. Freaking. James.

And she thought that maybe—just maybe—she might not be falling in love with him. Because she might be already there.

He pulled her into the crowd, where they were swallowed up by the stream of people heading toward the ride entrance. It didn't take long for the kids mixed with tourists to recognize Wyatt. Soon he was signing autographs and posing for pictures once more.

Tamera kept her distance, content to watch Wyatt from afar. Her fingers kept straying to her lips, as though reminding her that the kisses had been real. What had happened to swearing off men forever? She laughed. That was definitely out the window. She wanted to be with Wyatt.

A woman appeared at the edge of the crowd, her swollen belly pushing against the blue fabric of her sundress. Blonde curls cascaded down her back, but her face was swollen and red from the heat. She hobbled forward and Tamera cocked her head to one side. Something about the woman looked familiar, but she couldn't quite place it.

"Wyatt," the woman called, raising a hand.

Wyatt glanced around, clearly trying to locate the voice. His eyes found Tamera's, and she pointed to the pregnant woman in the sundress. She was a fan and hoping for an autograph, just like everyone else in the park.

Wyatt followed the direction of Tamera's finger and his gaze landed on the woman. His entire face went ashen, the color draining right out of it. Tamera rose, concern making her blood pump harder.

"Uh, sorry guys," Wyatt said, holding up his hands to the crowd around him. "That's all I have time for right now."

A chorus of groans met this announcement. Tamera walked toward Wyatt, her steps quick. He hadn't told any of his fans *no* all day.

The woman folded her arms and smirked, waiting for Wyatt to reach her. Tamera was almost to them as well. She could just hear Wyatt's soft words.

"Becky," he said. "What are you doing here?"

Becky. The ex. Tamera quickened her pace, feeling snakes of tension coil and leap in her stomach.

"What do you think I'm doing here?" Becky's tone was full of venom. She rested her hands on her protruding stomach and smirked up at Wyatt. "I'm here to collect child support, Daddy."

Chapter Twenty

A strange roaring filled Wyatt's ears—one that seemed to have drowned out Becky's words. He stared down at his ex and blinked, as though that would make the nightmare before him disappear.

"No," he said, glancing at her round belly. "That's not possible." One hundred thousand percent not possible, unless an immaculate conception had occurred.

"I can show you just how real this stomach is back at my hotel."

He heard a gasp and whipped around. Tamera stood behind him, her face bright red and fists clenched at her sides.

Wyatt took a step toward her, reaching out, but she shrank back.

How was this happening again? Hadn't Becky destroyed enough of his life already?

"She's lying," he said desperately, pleading with Tamera to believe him. He glared at Becky. "Tell her you're lying."

Becky ran a hand through her hair. Three inches of dark roots led to hair that had once been bleached blonde, but now looked more brassy. "I assure you, this baby is no lie."

"It's not mine!" Wyatt yelled. A few tourists glanced over at them, and he lowered his voice. "You know we never..."

Becky popped her gum and shrugged. "I'm due next month. We only broke up six months ago. You do the math."

Tamera backed away, shaking her head back and forth furiously. "I can't believe this is happening," she muttered.

Wyatt reached for Tamera, but she took another step back. "I don't know what's happening," he said desperately. He gesture to Becky. "There's no way that kid is mine."

"Apparently the only kind of men I attract are cheaters." Tamera gave a hollow laugh. "Is this the real reason why you traded to the Coyotes—to get away from your responsibilities?"

"Trust me, this is the first I'm hearing about this," Wyatt said. He reached for her hand, but Tamera backed away. Tears glistened in her eyes. Each one felt like a punch to Wyatt's heart.

"I'll find my own way home," Tamera said, her voice thick.

"Tamera—"

She strode quickly away, not looking back. Wyatt took a step forward, ready to run after her. But Becky's voice stopped him cold.

"If you chase after her, I'll ruin this lovely little PR opportunity the Coyotes have going for them and make a very big, very uncomfortable scene for you."

Wyatt froze, his blood suddenly turning to ice. The steely glint in Becky's eyes said she wasn't lying. Making a scene wouldn't just be disastrous for Wyatt, but for the entire team. For McKinley, who was working so hard to turn them into winners. For Luke, who'd done nothing but help Wyatt since he arrived in California. For Tyrone, who'd been a friend when Wyatt desperately needed one.

He couldn't let Becky throw her little tantrum for everyone to see. After he made Becky leave, he'd go find Tamera and insist she hear him out.

"Let's go somewhere private." Wyatt strode back to the alcove where minutes before he'd been kissing Tamera. Allowing Becky into this secret space felt wrong, but he didn't know where else they'd have a moment of privacy. His mouth filled with the bitter taste of fury.

He hated that Becky was here. Hated that he was now using the private alcove with so many pleasant memories for such an unpleasant moment.

Wyatt folded his arms and glared at his ex, trying to avoid staring at her stomach. "Start talking. We both know that baby isn't mine."

She glared and smoothed her hands over her rounded stomach. "You were too much of a choir boy for that, true. Which is why I know you'll help me now."

It felt like thinking through mud, but slowly the puzzle pieces began to fall into place, presenting a very hazy picture. "It's Drew's, isn't it?"

Becky's heavily made-up eyes lowered and she took a step forward. "It doesn't have to be his. We were good together, Wyatt." She reached up, threading her fingers through his hair and leaning in. He turned his head and her lips landed on his cheek.

"You think I'm, what—going to take you back and raise the kid as my own?" Wyatt asked incredulously.

She folded her arms, and the angry glint told him he was walking a very dangerous tightrope—one that might very soon snap.

"I want to get back together. I could move here, to California." She let out a hollow laugh. "It's not like I can cheer this season. They've already fired me from the Vigilantes. I'm sure Drew had something to do with that."

"Why aren't you in Texas, telling him all this?"

Becky's face hardened and more of the pieces clicked into place. She'd already gone to Drew. He'd turned her away.

"You've always wanted a family." Her hands snaked their way up Wyatt's chest, around his neck. Caressing. Entrapping. "No one would ever have to know the truth. We could buy a little house and settle down. Me and the baby could travel with you to away games and cheer you on from the stands. The media would love it. Think how much that publicity would help the Coyotes."

Wyatt pushed her hands away, fury making it hard to think rationally. He had to handle this in a way that would minimize any damage Becky might try and cause. "Stop. This is insane."

Tears welled in Becky's green eyes. Back when they were dating, Wyatt had always caved to her demands at the first hint of crying. But not anymore.

She wrapped her arms around her stomach and stared up at him with luminescent eyes. "You loved me once. You can love me again."

Wyatt shook his head. "I'm sorry, Becky. That's over."

Laughter floated over from the Jurassic Park ride and Wyatt flinched. If this conversation was somehow made public, it could ruin the reputation he'd somehow kept intact despite Drew's best efforts. Despite all the sacrifices and compromises Wyatt had made.

Would Tamera really leave the park without him? Did she really believe the lies Becky was telling?

"Please, Wyatt." Becky threw herself at him, pressing her body close. He felt the bulge of her stomach and his own churned with acid. The evidence of her infidelity burned.

"No," he said forcefully. "Why are you here, Becky?"

Her eyes hardened. He knew in that moment the games were over and the real Becky had showed up to play. "I need money."

Wyatt snorted. He shouldn't be surprised that this was what her visit was about. Fame and fortune had been more important to her than anything else. It had taken a while to realize that was probably why she'd cheated on him with Drew—the quarterback was the star of the team, after all. "Then go talk to your baby daddy."

"No one knows he's my baby daddy except you, me, and the coach."

Wyatt shifted from foot to foot as he realized she was right. The team had of course known that things were tense between Wyatt and Becky. That they'd broken up. But Drew's involvement in the whole thing had been kept under wraps. Coach had said the situation would only divide the team, and Wyatt had reluctantly agreed.

"But everyone knows you and I were together," Becky continued, rubbing her stomach with both hands. "If I went to the press, everyone would assume this baby is yours."

A stone fell in Wyatt's stomach, and he suddenly was having a hard time breathing. "We kept our relationship private. Only a couple of magazines even reported on our relationship." Or its demise.

A wicked grin stretched across Becky's face. "We didn't keep it private from the team. Drew has been busy since you left." She lifted a shoulder in a delicate shrug. "He hasn't said anything about me, of course, but he's let a few hints drop here and there about the kind of guy you really are. They're all on his side. If I tell them this baby is yours, and you won't take responsibility, they'll back me up in the press."

Wyatt's vision was going hazy around the corners as he struggled to breathe. "What are you saying?"

"I want five hundred thousand dollars for my silence. Wire me the money and I won't sell an exposé to some tabloid for that amount."

Wyatt choked, leaning forward. "You can't be serious."

"Trust me, I am. I just got fired. I have no medical insurance, no education, and no idea how I'm going to support myself now that I can't cheer. I have eighteen years of expenses ahead of me, not to mention college and eventually a wedding for this baby."

"Then ask Drew to pay." Why was she doing this?

Why was Tamera taking Becky's word over his?

"No one would believe me if I said Drew was the father," Becky said. "No one knows we were together. I have nothing to threaten him with."

"Get a paternity test. Make him pay child support."

"That takes time." Her eyes hardened. "I need money now. My medical bills are piling up and the delivery's going to make things even worse."

He couldn't believe she was even going there. He pointed a finger to the crowd swarming outside the alcove. "I think you should leave. Now."

Her voice rose as she shifted from foot to foot. "Are you sure that's what you want, Wyatt? One phone call and it'll be headline news tomorrow."

She might, but five hundred thousand dollars to pay for a consequence he hadn't earned? No way. "Then I'll demand a paternity test."

"Your reputation will be shredded before we ever get the results. By the time you get a judge to sign the order, it'll be too close to delivery to risk the procedure until after the baby's born. And that's not going to happen for at least five weeks."

Wyatt stared into her eyes, refusing to blink. She stared back, but she bit her lip—a sign of hesitation.

There was no way she'd go to the press. In the end, it would hurt her more than anyone once the lie came out.

Becky was bluffing. And Wyatt wasn't about to let her pull him into any more of her tangled webs.

"Go back to Drew," Wyatt said firmly. "Tell him if he voluntarily pays child support, you'll sign something promising not to go to the press. You're scared and that's understandable. But I'm not the answer to your problem. We're not together anymore." He pointed to where Tamera had stormed off only minutes ago. "I have feelings for someone else, and you very well may have ruined any chance I have with her."

Becky's eyes glistened with tears—real ones this time, if Wyatt wasn't mistaken. "Drew doesn't care about me or the baby. I'm sorry, Wyatt. I never should've cheated on you. I was scared by how much I loved you." She held up a hand, motioning to herself. "You can have any girl in the world. Why would you want me? I was so insecure. The other cheerleaders were always prettier and thinner and better than me. They would've jumped at the chance to date you."

Wyatt looked away. Seven months ago, the sight of Becky's tears would've had him jumping through whatever hoop she placed before him. But not anymore. What he had with Tamera—what they were beginning to build—was more real than his entire relationship with Becky.

He hoped she hadn't ruined that for good.

"I can't be what you need anymore," Wyatt said.

Her eyes glinted with the challenge. "I think you can."

Becky's hands snaked behind his head and pulled his lips to hers before he realized what was happening. Her kiss was hard and Wyatt wrenched himself away, furious. He stared at Becky, his chest heaving as he bit back the words he wants to hurl at her.

Becky's arms darkened and she folded her arms defensively. "So that's it, then?"

He ran a hand through his hair in disbelief. Had that seriously just happened? "Please go."

She shoved an angry finger in his face. "You'll regret this, Wyatt James." Then she disappeared into the crowd outside the alcove.

Wyatt slumped against the wall, letting his head fall back. His mind reeled at what had just happened. Becky was pregnant with Drew's child. Drew, who was also Tamera's best friend. Tamera, who thought Wyatt was abandoning his pregnant ex-girlfriend.

He fumbled for his phone and placed a call to Tamera. A lump welled up in his throat, but he swallowed it back. The phone rang and rang. Just when he was certain she wouldn't pick up, a click sounded on the other end of the line.

Wyatt pushed away from the wall. "Tamera—"

"Please don't call me anymore, Wyatt."

"She was lying," he said desperately. "We never even slept together. It's *Drew's* baby, Tamera. Not mine."

A hollow laugh filled the line, and he felt as though his heart was being squeezed into dust.

"Don't even go there with me." Her voice rose until she was practically shouting. "I've put up with a lot of back-and-forth with you and Drew, but I can't believe you would even go there now."

"So that's it?" Wyatt demanded. "All the time we've spent together means nothing to you? Drew's word wins out in the end?"

"I knew I was a bad judge of character." Tamera's voice wobbled, sending another dagger into his heart. "I just didn't realize how bad until now. Goodbye, Wyatt."

And the line went dead.

Chapter Twenty-One

Tamera's shoulders sagged in relief as the driver she'd called on a ride share app pulled up in front of her condo. She quickly wiped her tears and thanked him before climbing out of the vehicle. So much for a fun-filled day at Universal Studios. What a disaster.

Wyatt's ex-girlfriend was pregnant. And he was trying to say the baby was Drew's. She felt numb, as though her body refused to feel anymore as a defense mechanism. She didn't know who to believe. Wyatt seemed like a good guy—one she'd maybe even loved. But she'd lived with Drew for twelve weeks. He wouldn't abandon his pregnant mistress.

Would he?

Tamera trudged up the stairs to her condo. Confusion hung over her like a fog. Maybe she'd been too hasty in leaving the park. Didn't Wyatt at least deserve the opportunity to tell his side of the story?

But she was so tired of sides. Sick to death of he said/she said situations. They always ended with Tamera trying to pick out fact from fiction. Right now, all she wanted to do was crawl into bed and cry herself to sleep.

She paused at the top of the stairs, surprised to see someone standing in front of her door. A girl with long brown hair, the same color as Tamera's, was examining her nails. She wore shorts that could be classified as microscopic and held an oversized bag in the crook of one arm.

Well, so much for hitting rock bottom. Apparently there were still a few feet left to fall.

Tamera took a step backward, ready to run down the stairs. What was her sister doing here? She so couldn't deal with this right now. But the step creaked beneath her feet and Katie turned around.

"Tamera?" she called.

Tamera closed her eyes and cursed. Stupid stairs. Stupid noise that gave her away to her stupid sister. She didn't have the emotional bandwidth to deal with one more betrayal tonight. If Katie was here to tell her she was pregnant...

Katie put a hand on one hip. "I can see you hiding."

So much for escaping. Tamera sighed and walked up the last few stairs, mentally preparing for battle. "Katie. What are you doing here?"

"I came to see you, silly." Katie held out her arms and Tamera reluctantly went into them for a brittle hug.

"Where have you been?" Katie asked as Tamera unlocked her front door. "I've been waiting here for almost an hour."

No comment on Tamera's splotchy, tear-stained face. No concern for her well-being. "I was out."

Katie rolled her eyes. "Yeah, I figured out that much." She followed Tamera inside and tossed her purse on the couch, then sank down beside it. "You okay? It looks like you've been crying."

Tamera paused, then set her own purse on the counter. Katie hadn't asked if she was okay in a few years at least. What was her game? "I'm fine."

"You don't look fine."

Tamera ignored the comment. Instead, she grabbed a bottle of wine from the fridge and poured herself a glass. She could already tell that this conversation was going to require the extra help. She poured a glass for Katie as well—she was a happy drunk and that might work in Tamera's favor tonight. "This is a surprise. California's pretty far from Texas."

"Oh, you know." Katie accepted the glass of wine, avoiding

Tamera's gaze. "Everyday life is such a bore after the Bahamas. We decided to take a weekend trip. Sort of an extended honeymoon."

Yeah, Tamera wasn't touching that topic of conversation with a ten foot pole. She took a sip of her wine instead.

"Caleb went for a run," Katie continued. "He wanted to come and say hi, but I told him I needed some time with just me and my sister."

Tamera couldn't help it—she snorted and set her wine glass on the coffee table.

Katie's mouth turned down in a pout. "You don't have to be rude."

"Me?" Tamera shook her head in disbelief. "You stole my boyfriend, made me the maid of honor at your wedding, and now you're flying halfway across the country to rub it in my face. What's going on?"

Katie looked away, the tips of her ears turning red. She took a sip of her wine, avoiding Tamera's gaze. "It sounds so bad when you put it like that."

Tamera pinched the bridge of her nose. "I've had a pretty craptastic day. Get to the point." Whatever Katie was here for—a pregnancy announcement, to ask for money, maybe just to share more photos of the honeymoon—Tamera wanted her to get it over with and leave so she could go back to crying over Wyatt. She eyed the mostly full bottle of wine. It would pair nicely with an all-night binge-watching session.

Katie's eyes welled up with tears, startling Tamera almost as much as her arrival.

"Whoa," Tamera said, patting Katie's back. "What's wrong?"

"I think Caleb's already losing interest," Katie whispered. "I thought our honeymoon would be magical, but I never had his full attention."

I told you so was on the edge of Tamera's tongue, but she bit it hard, refusing to let the words slip out. For better or worse, Katie was her sister and she was hurting.

"Did you catch him with another woman?" Tamera asked cautiously. Had she seen the texts he'd sent Tamera and come to confront her?

She should've told Katie immediately.

Katie shook her head. "No, nothing that obvious. But his eyes would follow other women on the beach, or he'd make flirtatious comments to the waitress at dinner, or I'd be talking to him and he'd be on his phone. Just little things, but they have me worried. He's really good at hiding stuff, you know?"

Yeah, Tamera did know. Because he'd hid his relationship with Katie for a year. How was Tamera supposed to handle this?

This is so not what she had envisioned doing tonight. She and Wyatt were supposed to be cuddled close against the cooling night air, standing in line for the Simpson's Ride and talking to fans. She grabbed her wine glass and took a sip.

"I can't help but wonder..." Katie shot Tamera a sideways glance. "Well, he cheated once, you know? Maybe he'll do it again."

"You know what they say—once a cheater, always a cheater." Tamera kept her voice even and held Katie's gaze, refusing to blink or look away.

Katie broke eye contact first. She sniffed and looked down at her own glass of wine. "At first, it was about winning," she whispered. "I was so annoyed that once again, the guy I liked went for you over me."

Anger shot waves of heat up Tamera's spine. "When he asked for my number, I came to you and said I wouldn't go out with him if you didn't want me to. You laughed and said you could have a guy ten times hotter than him, and that I could take his call or not take his call, because it didn't matter to you."

Katie laughed darkly. "And what was I supposed to do, Tamera? Confess how big of a crush I had on Caleb and beg you to let me have a shot?"

"I would've let you." Tamera threw up her hands. "But you never told me, Katie. And then you stabbed me in the back in the worst possible way. I wouldn't treat my worst enemy the way you've treated me. We're supposed to be sisters."

"I know." Katie's words were thick with suppressed emotion. "And I know I shouldn't have come here, either. But I didn't know where else to go."

Tamera folded her arms tightly across her stomach. It ached with the pain of this conversation, and she wished she could reverse the clock and wish Katie back to Texas. "Do you love him?"

Katie's eyes widened and Tamera caught the sparkle of tears. "What?"

"It's a simple question. Do. You. Love. Him?"

"I..." Katie's shoulders slumped. "Maybe. I don't know."

She hadn't known if she was in love, but she'd married him anyway just to hurt Tamera. Another stab of betrayal.

"I was so caught up in everything, you know?" Katie continued. "Someone had finally chosen me over you. It felt ... well, it felt amazing, to be honest. But I didn't mean to hurt you. I'm so sorry, Tamera."

Tamera blinked, not sure she wanted to hear Katie's apology. Not sure she was ready to accept it. But she did know one thing—she couldn't hurt Katie the way she'd been hurt. Slowly, Tamera opened her phone to the texts from Caleb and handed it to Katie.

Katie's eyes scanned the texts as the color drained from her face.

"I should've told you immediately," Tamera said. "But I was ... I don't know. Shocked, I guess? You were on your honeymoon, for heaven's sake. It wasn't like I expected him to reach out."

Katie rose, grabbing her purse. "So it's still you he wants."

Tamera rose as well. "He doesn't know what he wants. That's the problem. He's not good enough for you, Katie. Both of us deserve someone better."

The phone buzzed and Katie gasped. She threw the phone at Tamera and headed toward the door.

"Katie!" Tamera grabbed the phone, quickly reading the text.

Katie didn't want me to come with her to see you. Maybe we can meet up tonight after she's asleep?

Tamera closed her eyes, silently cursing Caleb.

"A month!" Katie yelled. "We've barely been married a month and already he's going back to you."

"I told him to be faithful." Tamera brandished her phone like a weapon. "It's all right here in black and white. Just read the stupid texts."

"It doesn't matter." Katie threw open the door. "Thanks for nothing."

Tamera stared, her hands curling into fists as her bruised and battered heart took yet another hit. "You've got to be kidding me."

"What do you want me to say, Tamera? My husband would still rather be with you."

So much for apologizing. Tamera blinked back the angry tears forming in her eyes. "I have tried so hard to be a good sister. I let you plan my dream wedding and didn't say a word. I let you marry my groom and smiled for the camera. I caught your bridal bouquet and didn't make a scene."

"Yeah, you've been a freaking saint." Katie pointed at the cell phone. "If you didn't tell me about the texts, what else are you hiding?"

Tamera threw up her hands and shook her head in disbelief. "I'm done here."

"That makes two of us then. Have a nice life." Katie slammed the door behind her, rattling the frame so hard that a clock fell off the wall and crashed to the floor. The protective glass cracked, sending spiderwebs all across the face.

Tamera dropped to the floor and stared at the clock, no longer able to hold back the tears.

Her phone buzzed again, skittering across the hardwood floors. Tamera set the clock on the ground and crawled over to her phone, picking it up to find another text from Caleb.

Still keep your spare key behind the loose brick?

No—Tamera had moved it not long after she and Caleb broke up. She texted him back with shaking fingers.

I showed Katie the texts.

A string of curses soon came through. Tamera deleted the texts with shaking fingers, then blocked the number.

What a mess.

Chapter Twenty-Two

Dragging himself to practice the next day took a concerted effort. Wyatt texted Tamera three times while getting ready, and again on the drive, but she never responded.

He was just pulling into the stadium parking lot when his phone rang. He pulled to a jerky stop in a parking space and fumbled to answer it, his heart momentarily lifting until he saw Natalie's name on the caller ID.

He leaned his head back against the headrest, then answered the call, doing his best to keep his voice light. "Hey, sis."

"Anything you want to tell me about, big brother?"

Wyatt blinked, surprised by her accusatory tone of voice. "I don't think so."

"Because the article I'm staring at right now says I'm going to be an aunt. Are you freaking kidding me? You chose Becky to be the mother to your progeny? You're an idiot."

"Whoa." Wyatt sat up and put the phone on speaker, then opened up his web browser. "Becky is pregnant, but the baby isn't mine. We never ... it's just not possible, okay?"

Natalie's heavy breathing echoed across through the line. It would've made Wyatt smile if he wasn't so upset. He could imagine how she looked right now—sprawled across her bed, staring at the ceiling as her sandy blonde hair splayed around her. "You swear it?"

"I swear. You know me better than that."

"I thought I did, but the article ... I don't know. It messed with my head."

Wyatt paused, finding the article in question. He massaged his eyes, that sick feeling back in his gut. The photographer had caught Becky kissing him and the angle made it look like Wyatt was responding.

"Unbelievable," he muttered.

"What's going on? Mom and Dad are going to flip out when they see this."

"Becky is insane, that's what's going on." Wyatt sighed deeply, closing the web browser in disgust.

Tamera would see that article, if she hadn't already. It was inevitable with how much time she spent online. The stupid article was probably why she wasn't answering his texts. He had a sinking feeling she'd already seen the picture, read the lies, and believed every word.

"Explain," Natalie demanded.

So Wyatt told her about what had happened the day before while Natalie listened intently.

"Do you think Becky had the photographer planned all along?" Natalie asked.

Wyatt got out of his truck and grabbed his duffel bag. He'd better hurry, or he'd be late to practice. "I don't know. On the one hand I wouldn't put it past her. On the other hand, she has nothing to hold over me now."

"This will blow over," Natalie said. "The article is all speculation. This isn't even one of the good tabloids."

"I don't think that will help me with Tamera," Wyatt said quietly. He nodded at a teammate across the parking lot and slowed his pace a little so they wouldn't run into each other before he finished his phone call.

"Wyatt, give the girl a break. I'm your own sister and I called to yell at you, worried the rumors were true. You did date Becky for six months —it's not a stretch to believe a baby is within the realm of possibility."

The hairs on his arms prickled in outrage. "I've done nothing but try and earn Tamera's trust from the very beginning. I can't have a relationship with someone who's constantly questioning my motives."

"I agree," Natalie said easily. "Geez, don't bite off my head. I'm just saying she was taken off guard. Probably a little shocked at what was happening. Let her cool off a bit, then explain everything."

"But—"

"Do you like her?" Natalie demanded.

Wyatt entered the corridor leading to the locker room and lowered his voice so it wouldn't echo. "What do you mean? Of course I like her."

"I mean do you *like*-like her. Does she make your tummy get butterflies? Do you get all hot and bothered when she's in the room?"

Wyatt rolled his eyes, but couldn't deny the quiver he felt at the mere mention of Tamera.

"Is she the last thing you think about before falling asleep, and the first thing you think about when you wake up?" Natalie continued.

Wyatt lifted his duffel bag higher on his shoulder, suddenly feeling very uncomfortable.

"I'll take your silence as a yes. I watched *Eye in the Sky*, Wyatt—I think Tamera's the real deal. So give her a chance, okay?"

A chance. He felt like he'd already given Tamera so many, and the thought of putting his heart on the line one more time was agonizing.

Wyatt glanced up at the locker room door. "I've got to go, Natalie. I'm at practice."

"Think about what I said," Natalie said, then hung up without saying goodbye.

Practice was exactly what Wyatt needed. He put all his energy into the drills, even earning a compliment from McKinley on his hard work. And all the while, Natalie's words swirled in his head. Was Tamera's reaction only natural? She'd been betrayed in the worst possible way by her boyfriend and sister. Was close friends with Drew, who was a pathological liar and cheat. That would mess with anyone's head.

As he walked back to the locker room after practice, he knew he would put his heart on the line one last time for Tamera. He had to talk to her. She deserved the truth, even if she slammed the door in his face. And he needed to know he'd tried.

Wyatt quickly got dressed after his shower while Tyrone gave him the side-eye.

"You okay, man?" Tyrone asked.

Wyatt blew out a breath. "Nothing I can't handle."

"I saw the article," Tyrone ventured carefully. "Tough break. That's a lot to take in."

Wyatt shut his locker with more force than strictly necessary. "The kid's not mine. But I know who is the father, and I don't think he'll be eager to come forward and set the story straight. Now Tamera won't talk to me." He ran a hand over his head, agitated. "Things were going really well yesterday."

"She seems really nice," Tyrone said. "Smokin' hot, too, which doesn't hurt any."

"Unfortunately, she also has a lot of baggage and hangups. And Becky showing up yesterday didn't help at all. Tamera won't take my texts or phone calls."

Tyrone shrugged. "We're all a little screwed up deep down, right? If you like her, go explain. Even if she still calls it quits, at least you'll know you tried."

Wyatt nodded, grabbing his bag. He'd made up his mind before this conversation even began. "I've got to go."

"Good luck," Tyrone called as Wyatt raced from the locker room.

He was halfway down the corridor when Luke stepped out of his office and the two nearly collided. Wyatt skidded to a halt, barely managing to avoid bowling Luke over.

"Sorry about that," Wyatt said, breathing hard.

Luke laughed, clapping him on the back. "In a hurry?"

"Kind of."

"I won't keep you, then. But I just saw the final cuts of all three commercials and I'm really excited to air them. Season ticket sales are going to explode once they hit the air." Luke walked away, calling over his shoulder, "Great job, Wyatt."

"Uh, thanks," Wyatt said. His commercials hadn't sucked?

Maybe the universe was finally working in his favor. And maybe his luck would hold for one more conversation.

Wyatt climbed in his truck and drove as fast as traffic would allow to

Tamera's condo. He pulled into the parking lot, surprised to see Tamera placing a suitcase in the trunk of an unfamiliar car.

He screeched into a parking spot and jumped out of the cab of his truck. "Tamera!"

She shut the trunk and looked up, surprise crossing her features for the briefest moment before her expression turned carefully blank.

He jogged across the parking lot and stopped a few feet away. "I'm sorry," he said.

She folded her arms. "I saw the articles."

It was hard not to curse. Wyatt put a fist to his mouth and took a deep breath. "Becky kissed me. If that photographer had taken the photo a second later, it would've shown me pushing her away."

Tamera let out a bitter laugh and shook her head. "Typical."

"I'm telling the truth."

Tears filled her eyes and she blinked quickly. "I have tried to give you the benefit of the doubt—over and over again. But your stories are seriously starting to skirt the edge of believability."

"Becky needed money," Wyatt said desperately. He could feel Tamera slipping away. Feel her past baggage blinding her to the truth. And he didn't know how to fix it. "The whole team in San Antonio knew we were together—the players, the cheerleaders, the coaches. But no one knew about her and Drew."

"Why?" she demanded. "Why did you keep quiet about what happened?"

"Because I was trying to salvage my career. I told you that I didn't want to hurt the team." He held his hands out imploringly. "I know you've been hurt before, Tamera. But I'm not here to cause you pain. Please."

She held his eyes, and for a moment, he felt a glimmer of hope—a desperate and wild belief that they could work through this.

"I want to believe you. But I can't trust my own judgment. You seem like a good guy. When we're together, I feel like you're telling the truth." She shrugged, and he wanted to pull her into his arms and kiss her breathless. Assure her he would do anything for her. Fight for her.

"Please," he whispered.

She blinked and looked down, fumbling for the car door and sliding inside. "If I don't leave now, I'll miss my flight."

Wyatt placed his hands against the window and she rolled it down. "Where are you going?"

Now she was definitely avoiding his gaze. "San Antonio. Drew invited me to visit for a few days. I need to get out of L.A."

The car started moving, but Wyatt stayed put, his feet frozen to the blacktop. Drew. He was losing out to the quarterback once more, but this time the prize was infinitely more precious. No, not a prize—a person. Someone he loved.

"Don't go," he called after the vehicle. "Tamera. Tamera!"

She poked her head out of the window. "I'm sorry," she said. And then the car disappeared down the road, taking the woman he loved with it.

Chapter Twenty-Three

~~~

Tamera let the music of the club pulse through her, giving herself over to the beat as she danced with Drew. The dance floor crackled with energy as couples laughed and drank and kissed. The strobe lights caught Drew's hair, highlighting the brown in his dirty blond.

Wyatt had come after her, and still she'd driven away. Tamera closed her eyes, pain slicing through her once more. But his claims were so ridiculous. She wanted to believe him, but she'd been wrong so many times before.

So why did her heart keep screaming that she was giving her loyalties to the wrong man? Why did she ache to hop the next plane back to L.A.?

Drew nudged her chin with one finger, forcing her to look up into his dark eyes. "You're in your head again," he said.

She'd spilled the whole story to him last night, after he picked her up at the airport and drove her to the hotel. Drew had called Wyatt all kinds of names and insisted Tamera was making the right decision. When she got to the part where Wyatt insisted Becky's baby must be Drew's, he'd laughed darkly and said that seemed like the kind of story a desperate man told. But throughout the entire conversation, Tamera couldn't help but think that Wyatt had never said anything bad against Drew. He'd accused him of lying, but he hadn't insisted she break off their friendship. He didn't waste his breath hurling insults. But Drew couldn't wait to throw digs Wyatt's way.

"Sorry," Tamera said, forcing herself to smile brightly at Drew. "It's been a week."

The article about Becky's pregnancy hadn't made much of a splash. Tamera spent most of last night trolling social media after she checked into the hotel, but the story had only been picked up by one or two minor blogs. No one seemed to care that Wyatt James and some random cheerleader may or may not be having a baby. Their relationship had never been public and news of Wyatt's trade was still the hotter topic on the web. But that hadn't stopped Tamera from reading every comment proclaiming what an adorable couple they made and offering up congratulations.

"You think too much," Drew said with a sly grin. "I don't think I should leave you alone tonight. Let's cancel your hotel room. You can come back to my place."

Pinpricks of unease made their way up Tamera's spine and she took a cautious step back. "I don't think that's a good idea."

Drew rested his hands on her waist, pulling her toward him. "You mean a lot to me, Tamera."

"You mean a lot to me, too. As a friend." She emphasized the last word as she pulled away, avoiding eye contact.

"Don't be like that." He grabbed her hips again, swaying to the beat of the music. "We were great together on *Eye in the Sky*. Everyone expects us to hook up. Let's give the fans what they want. That should make your agent happy."

"Drew." She pushed against his chest, her own tightening in fear. "I think you've had a little too much to drink. Let go."

"You are such a tease." He dropped his hands and scowled. "I've done everything I can to be a good friend to you. I took you under my wing on *Eye in the Sky*."

She gave a disbelieving laugh. "Uh, we both know I was the brains of that duo. You ruined my game."

He continued doggedly on, ignoring her. "When your ex freaked you out, who flew across the country to comfort you?"

"I never asked you to do that."

"You owe me." He raised a finger and pointed it at her face.

She slapped his finger away roughly, heat flowing through her. "I don't owe you anything."

He swore, his face turning red. "Then what have I been wasting my time for?"

Her mouth fell open as she stared at Drew, like she was seeing him for the first time. She'd seen glimpses of this side in his diary room interviews but thought it was all part of the game.

Wyatt was right—Drew had been the bad guy all along.

"Did you lie to get Wyatt transferred to the Coyotes?" Tamera demanded.

Drew rolled his eyes. "Do we have to talk about that again? Let's dance."

He tried to grab her hips once more, but she swatted his hands away. "Answer the freaking question."

His eyes hardened and he took a step closer, lowering his voice. "Yes, I lied. Becky and I had been seeing each other for months. When Wyatt found out, I couldn't let him stick around. The team would've looked at me differently if they knew."

She shook her head in horror. "The baby."

"What?"

"Becky's baby," she practically screamed. "Wyatt is right. You're the father."

Drew looked around quickly, then grabbed her arm and hauled her off the dance floor. She yanked her arm from his grasp, but followed him out of the club and into the cool night air.

"You are so naive," Drew sneered, his lips turning up in disgust. "Of course the baby's mine. But I'm not about to let a kid ruin my career."

"I can't believe what I'm hearing." She ran a shaky hand through her hair. "You tried to ruin Wyatt's life. He's been the good guy all along. I was an idiot not to see it sooner."

"You and me belong together," Drew shot back. "Everyone sees it. Why do you keep fighting the inevitable?"

"Oh no." She held up her hands and walked backward. "We're done, Drew."

His face darkened and he grabbed her arm. "I never wanted Becky. She was just a fling."

"Let go," Tamera said, feeling her palms grow clammy. She tugged, but Drew held on tight.

"When I met you on *Eye in the Sky*, I realized you were a girl I actually enjoyed talking to. Not just someone to mess around with in the bedroom. I want you so bad."

Tamera let out a shaky laugh, still trying to pull away. "And you thought the correct way to win me over was to ignore your responsibilities and abandon the mother of your child? To let a good guy get harassed by the press—to try and ruin his career—for something he didn't do?"

"Tamera." Drew's grip relaxed and his eyes grew soft in the moonlight—the puppy dog look he'd used on *Eye in the Sky* to manipulate others into doing what he wanted them to. "I'm sorry. I only lied because I was afraid of losing you."

She yanked her arm away and scrambled backward. "Well, congratulations, Drew. You've definitely lost me."

"Tamera!" Drew called.

She hurried back into the club and ducked into a hidden alcove. With trembling hands, she pulled her phone from her clutch and requested a ride through an app. A few moments later, Drew stormed past. Tamera shrank into the shadows, holding her breath until he was out of sight again.

Tears filled her eyes and her legs began to tremble. She sank into a crouch and dropped her head into her hands. Wyatt had asked her to trust him, but she'd left instead. What a horrible, awful mistake. In the moment it had felt wrong, but she'd ignored her gut and plowed forward. How would he ever forgive her?

A few minutes later, she ducked out of the club and into the car waiting for her.

"Where to?" the driver asked.

Tamera stared at him bleakly. "What?"

He gave her a puzzled frown. "You've got somewhere you want to go, right?"

She sniffed and wiped under her eyes. The hotel was only ten minutes away, but crying alone in a dark room didn't hold much appeal. She wanted someone to hold her and say everything would be alright. To assure her she wasn't irreparably broken and could fix her damaged relationship with Wyatt.

She wanted her sister.

The realization stunned her into giving the driver Katie's address. Soon he was dropping her off in front of a cute bungalow of whitewashed brick. Tamera thanked him and walked slowly up the front steps.

She stared at the door for a long time. Once upon a time, she and Katie had shared everything. They'd competed, yes. But they'd shared their joys and heartaches, too. They'd been each other's best friends. All that had changed when Tamera started dating Caleb.

She took a deep breath, then knocked. A few moments later, the door opened. Katie's hair was disheveled, as though she'd been asleep. Mascara was smudged under her eyes and she wore a ratty camisole and basketball shorts.

"Tamera." She rubbed at her eyes as though not quite believing them. "What are you doing here?"

"I guess I just needed my sister." Tamera's voice broke on the last word. Would Katie tell her to go away and never come back? "Can I come in?"

"Uh, sure." Katie opened the door wider and motioned her inside. Tamera entered, relief flowing through her.

The living room was dark, but Katie flipped on a light. It looked much the same as the last time Tamera had been here, barely more than a month ago. They'd spent five frustrating hours putting personalized wrappers on miniature candy bars as part of the wedding favors. White couches were still arranged around a barnwood coffee table. The television still sat on a hutch that Tamera had helped Katie refinish shortly before Caleb ruined everything.

"What are you doing in town?" Katie asked, grabbing a glass from the kitchen cupboard and turning on the faucet.

"I was visiting Drew." Tamera took a seat on the couch and accepted the glass of water Katie handed her.

"You look awful," Katie said, but there was an edge of satisfaction in her voice that stung. "What happened?"

Tears filled Tamera's eyes again and she shook her head quickly. "Please, can we not pick at each other tonight? I just ... I just need my sister."

Katie folded her arms. "I'm sitting right here."

"I'm sorry," Tamera choked out. She wiped under her eyes. "I should've told you about the texts immediately."

Katie looked down, playing with the hem of her shirt. "I probably wouldn't have believed you unless I saw the evidence for myself."

"I should've realized how overshadowed you felt," Tamera plowed on. "I should've listened to what you weren't saying as much as what you were all those times."

Katie's eyes softened and she scooted to the edge of the couch. "I'm sorry, too," she whispered, her eyes luminescent. "I should've told Caleb to take a hike the first time he made a move, but I was so flattered. And now ... oh, Tamera. I've made such a mess of things. Can you ever forgive me?"

"Of course," Tamera said. She held open her arms and Katie fell into them, the two of them crying and hugging. Tamera closed her eyes, relishing the realization that she had her little sister back.

"I never should've come to L.A.," Katie said. "I suck at apologizing. I swear I didn't plan on storming out in a rage."

Tamera laughed. "I should've been kinder when you showed up. I knew how hard it was for you to say you were sorry."

"I'm done competing with you." Katie sniffed, wiping under both eyes. "I just want us to be friends. Because I really, really need a friend right now."

"Me too," Tamera said. She looked around the dark bungalow. "Is Caleb still asleep?"

Katie's eyes darkened and she shook her head. "He's doing the music for a wedding tonight. I don't expect him home for another few hours at least."

So Katie had given him another chance. He was still living here, for better or worse, and Tamera was still going to have to deal with him at least sometimes.

"I know what you're thinking," Katie said, her voice tight. "I should've kicked him out. But he's my husband."

Tamera reached out and clasped Katie's hands in both of hers. "I support whatever decision you make."

Katie's lips turned up in a smile and she gave Tamera another hug. "Thank you. Now, tell me what's really going on. You're a total mess."

For the next hour, Tamera spilled out everything that had happened over the past month. When she'd finally told the whole story, Katie shook her head in disbelief.

"Wow," Katie said.

"I know."

"Honestly, I'm not surprised—Drew was kind of a creep on *Eye in the Sky*. I never really understood why the two of you were friends."

Tamera's mouth dropped open. "And you're just now telling me this?"

Katie held up her hands. "I'm sorry, okay? But I thought you'd bite my head off if I said anything at the wedding. Things were already so tense."

Tamera sank back against the couch cushions, trying to process this new information. "Wow."

"Wyatt seems like a good guy," Katie ventured.

"One of the best."

"So what are you going to do about it?"

Tamera took a deep breath. "I'm going back to L.A. And I'm going to try and win him back."

Chapter Twenty-Four

W yatt cursed and slammed his laptop lid shut. He leaned back in the uncomfortable hotel chair and rubbed his eyes. This script was going nowhere fast. Stupid writer's block.

The weekend had been awful. Imagining Tamera with Drew made him physically sick, but Wyatt couldn't get the image out of his head. He hadn't left his hotel in three days and it showed. The bed was unmade and dirty towels littered the floor, mixing in with the empty room service trays.

In two days, he'd see Tamera again whether he wanted to or not. He was closing on his house and knew she'd be there despite the turmoil their personal relationship was currently experiencing.

He wanted to hate Tamera. He'd put his heart on the line, begged her to stay, and she'd driven away without a backward glance. Wyatt wanted to be furious with her for not trusting him. But a bigger part of him wanted to wrap her in his arms and promise to spend the rest of his life proving to her she was worth loving. That not all men were out to hurt her. The baggage she carried must be so heavy, and he would gladly help lighten the load if she'd just let him.

A sharp rap sounded at the door and Wyatt looked up in surprise.

He'd put a *do not disturb* sign on his door and not even housekeeping had bothered him.

"Open up," came a cheerful voice. "Your sister's here to save the day."

The sound of his sister's voice had him scrambling to open the door. He flung it open and pulled Natalie into a tight hug. "What are you doing here?"

"Can't. Breathe," Natalie panted, pushing against his chest.

Wyatt dropped his arms and stepped back. Normally her antics would make him laugh, but tonight he couldn't summon up the energy.

"I thought you decided not to come until the semester was over," Wyatt said. "I should be all moved in by then."

Natalie tossed her sandy blonde hair, the same color as their mom's, over one shoulder and shut the door behind her. "This is a surprise visit to do damage control."

"What are you talking about?"

"Clearly you're depressed and wallowing over your admittedly horrendous luck." She sat gingerly on the edge of his bed, her nose wrinkling in disgust. "Gross, Wyatt. Let the maids in to clean occasionally. It looks like you haven't left in days."

Wyatt slumped into the uncomfortable desk chair, not meeting her eyes.

She groaned. "Yeah, hopping on that plane was definitely a good idea. Talk to me."

"What do you want me to say? I tried to explain, and she ran right into Drew's waiting arms." The second time he'd lost a woman to the quarterback. He'd thought last time had been painful, but it was nothing compared to this. He hadn't loved Becky. But his entire heart ached for Tamera. His feelings for her had snuck up on him so gradually, he hadn't realized what was happening until it was too late.

Natalie slugged him hard in the shoulder. "You are such a guy."

He rubbed his arm and scowled. "What's that supposed to mean?"

"It means you're an idiot." She sighed and absently began to straighten the items on his bedside table. "Of course she ran back to Drew. She's known him longer. He's safe and familiar—exactly the kind of scum she's used to dating."

Wyatt furrowed his brow. "You're making even less sense than usual."

Natalie rolled her eyes and placed one hand on her hip, reminding him vividly of their mother. "Tamera said so herself—she's always fallen for guys who are all wrong for her. She's dated the Drews and Calebs of the world her entire life. Now that she's faced with a Wyatt, she's scared."

"Huh?"

Natalie sighed dramatically and flopped back on the bed. "I know, I know—matters of the heart can be confusing. The point I'm trying to make is that Tamera has never felt for someone what she feels for you. And she's terrified it'll all blow up in her face if she moves forward. So when something happened that seemed, you know, explosion worthy, she ran for the hills."

Wyatt struggled to process what Natalie was saying. "You're saying she freaked out and left because she did believe me? She knew all along I was telling the truth?"

"Maybe. You'll have to talk to Tamera to find out for sure." Natalie lifted one shoulder in a delicate shrug. "What I'm saying is that I've never seen you this way over a girl."

That's because he'd never been in love before. The weeks following Becky's betrayal had been difficult, but more because of the situation than because he wanted her back. Wyatt rubbed his jaw, considering Natalie's words. He certainly hadn't felt like his heart had been been ripped out of his chest and stomped on with Becky, that was for sure. It hadn't hurt to breathe. To imagine a life without her.

"So what do I do about all this?" Wyatt said cautiously. "Tamera is in San Antonio with Drew right now. They've got history together."

"History we both know was built on manipulation and lies. Did you even pay attention to the show? He totally destroyed her game."

"Yeah, but it was a game."

"It showed his true colors," Natalie countered.

"So I'm supposed to ... what? Declare my undying love to her? Wave a magic wand and somehow make her forget all the lies and accusations she's heard against me?"

"Seriously, do I have to do all the work for you?" Natalie tossed her hair over one shoulder, a sure sign of annoyance. "Tamera needs to be reminded of who you really are. She needs to be shown the real Wyatt. The one she fell for, outside of all the rumors and speculations and evil quarterbacks trying to ruin your life."

"Sure. Because that will be so easy to show her."

"You know Tamera." Natalie's eyes softened and she leaned her chin in her hands, holding Wyatt's gaze. "Not the girl on *Eye in the Sky*. Or the woman who sells houses. Or even the actress who goes on auditions with Hollywood agents. You know *her*. And that's what you have to show her. That both of you have been real with each other. Take off the masks, throw all your cards on the table, and see if you can win the biggest game of your life."

Wyatt's breath quickened as he imagined confronting Tamera one last time and doing just that. He could almost imagine her eyes softening. Her body leaning toward his. Her lips caressing, tugging, opening.

He wanted Sunday afternoon movie marathons with her in his new home. He wanted to hold hands in the mall and argue over what to make for dinner. A life with Tamera was worth risking it all one last time.

Wyatt snapped his fingers together, an idea forming. "I think I know what to do."

"You're not going to put *Tamera, will you marry me?* on the JumboTron at the first pregame, are you? Because that's a little cheesy."

"Uh, no. I think a marriage proposal is a little premature." But maybe it wasn't as out of the question as Wyatt had feared. Maybe Natalie was right, and there was a way to salvage this.

"What's the plan then?" Natalie asked.

"Okay, here's what I'm going to do." He leaned forward, outlining his plan to Natalie. Her eyes grew wider with each word and she nodded enthusiastically.

"If that doesn't work, Tamera is insane. Oh my gosh, I'm dying. It's too perfect." Natalie clapped her hands together. "Chop chop, big brother. Let's get to work."

Chapter Twenty-Five

~∾∾~

The plane pulled to a stop and Tamera felt a rush of deja vu. Had it really only been six weeks since she'd last touched down in L.A.? Her mind had been filled with thoughts of Wyatt then, too.

Tamera turned her phone back on as passengers filed into the aisle. Soon her screen was filled with notifications. She clicked on the first one —a text from Katie.

Let me know when you've landed safely. Love ya, sis. Thanks for this weekend.

Tamera's broken heart put another piece of itself back together, and she quickly texted Katie back. Tamera hadn't been able to get an earlier flight out of San Antonio, so she'd spent the weekend with Katie, working on repairing their relationship. Tamera had only seen Caleb once. Their conversation had been awkward and uncomfortable, but Tamera had tried to keep things distant while still polite for Katie's sake. The twinge of betrayal was still there—it would take a while to fade completely, if ever—but as she spoke to Caleb, Tamera realized that it had lessened to a dull ache.

The weekend had been healing in so many ways. Whatever happened with Wyatt, Tamera would be okay. As much as it hurt to think about failing in her mission to win him back, Tamera knew it was time to start trusting herself. She knew it wasn't a change that would happen overnight. But she was also confident that in a year she'd look back at this moment and be proud of the progress she'd made.

She flicked over to the next text and saw it was from Hershel, her agent.

Audition at four p.m. today, he'd written, followed by an address.

Tamera glanced at her watch and gasped. It was already after two p.m. Her fingers flew over the screen as she texted Hershel back. **I've been on a plane and just barely got this. I'm not sure I can make the audition.**

She moved into the center aisle and was nearly off the plane when her phone rang again.

Do whatever you need to and make the audition. They really want you for the part.

I haven't even had time to read over the script.

You do great at cold readings. Trust me. This is one you don't want to miss.

Tamera chewed on her lip, then finally texted him back one letter. **K.**

It would be tight—no time to rush back to her condo and change clothes. She'd have to head to the audition straight from the airport. As Tamera waited in baggage claim for her suitcase, she sighed. What was the point? In the past month and a half, she'd been on four auditions and only received one callback.

She thought of Wyatt, his wide grin turning her insides to goo as he insisted that one day she'd make it. When Tamera's suitcase came around on the carousel, she took a deep breath and grabbed it, then headed to grab a ride. What was that saying—you missed one hundred percent of the shots you didn't take? She'd give the audition her best shot, despite the less than ideal circumstances.

In the car, Tamera tried to calm her jittery nerves by finally forcing herself to do something she'd been avoiding all weekend—text Wyatt.

I'm sorry. You were right. I should've trusted you all along. She stared at the words on the screen, feeling her heart somewhere in her throat as her entire body tingled with anticipation and worry. The words were so inadequate, but she didn't know how much more she wanted to say in a text. But calling him up would take more courage than she currently possessed. Hearing his voice would undo her already strained composure.

She took a deep breath and pushed send. A few minutes later, her phone dinged.

What happened? Wyatt asked.

She should've put on her big girl panties and just called him—it was so hard to tell tone in a text. **I'd rather tell you in person. Can you come over for dinner tonight? I have a lot of groveling to do.**

One nail made its way into her mouth as she held her breath, waiting for his response. She didn't have a plan B if he refused to come over. Maybe she'd show up at his hotel and refuse to leave until he heard her out? That seemed a little stalkerish. At least they'd see each other at the house closing, no matter what.

Finally, the text came. **Okay.** One word—not exactly an enthusiastic acceptance of her invitation, but she'd take what she could get.

Seven o'clock? she asked. **I've got an audition, but should be back by then.**

See you then.

She closed her phone and leaned her head back against the seat. Get through a blind audition, figure out what to make for dinner, then tell Wyatt she'd been wrong and beg for forgiveness from the love of her life. Easy-peasy.

The car pulled up to the address and Tamera's brow furrowed in confusion. The Coyotes stadium loomed above her, the lights aimed at the field just visible above the bleachers.

"Are you sure this is the right address?" Tamera asked.

"Yeah," the driver said.

"Uh, okay. Thanks."

Tamera got out of the car and walked into the stadium on trembling legs. Maybe Wyatt hadn't exaggerated about his poor performance in the commercials, and Luke had decided to bring in some actresses instead. So Tamera was going to—what? Dress up in a cheer skirt and shell top, then wave some pompoms for the camera? They must have dozens of actual cheerleaders to pick from who would do fine in front of the camera. Die-hard fans would spot an actress from a mile away.

The stadium corridors were empty and Tamera's heels echoed with each step. Metal doors were pulled down over the concession stand openings. Thick fabric coverings hid the food carts. It was strange to be here without a crush of fans and the distant roar of a cheering crowd. Kind of eerie.

A woman appeared underneath one of the concrete gates leading up to the stands. She was tall but thin, with long sandy blonde hair and a pretty smile. As Tamera got closer, she realized the woman looked young enough to still be in college.

"Hi," the woman said brightly, extending a hand.

"Hi," Tamera said, shaking the hand cautiously.

"You must be Tamera." The woman laughed. "What am I saying? Of course you are. I recognize you from *Eye in the Sky*. I'm a huge fan of that show. Anyway, come this way, please. The audition is right through here."

Tamera let the woman tug her through the gate. She kept chattering, not seeming to expect Tamera to do more than listen. They wove their way through the cushioned chairs next to the sideline.

"Here we are," the woman said. Tamera still didn't know her name.

Tamera raised an eyebrow, glancing at the pristine field of lush green grass. "The audition is on the field?"

"That's right," the woman said cheerfully. She pulled a stapled packet from the folder she carried and handed it to Tamera. "If you'll just head out to the field, we can start."

Tamera took the script, looking around for a casting director or another actor. Anyone who didn't look like an intern. "Uh, I don't know if my agent told you, but I haven't had time to read through the script."

The woman waved a hand through the air. "Not a problem. I'll be right over there." She pointed to a bench so far away, Tamera wondered how she'd be able to hear the audition. Tamera could project her voice pretty far, but that still seemed like an odd place to watch from.

"Okay." Tamera flipped through the script, not really seeing the words. "Who's reading the other part?"

"He'll be out in a minute. You can get started without him." The woman headed toward her faraway bench, apparently done answering questions.

"Okay then," Tamera muttered as she walked onto the field. She slipped out of her heels and left them on the sideline, acutely aware of the punctures they'd make in the field. Soft, cool grass tickled her feet as she stopped and shaded her eyes, trying to see the woman despite the glare from the afternoon sun. "Is this okay?"

The woman held up her hand in an *okay* sign. "Perfect."

"So you don't want me to wait for the other guy?"

"Nope," the woman called. "Start reading. He'll be here soon enough."

This was definitely the weirdest audition Tamera had ever been on. She focused on the page and silently read the first stage direction.

A beautiful woman steps onto the football field. Her posture is defensive, arms folded and eyes cautious. She's scared to give the hero the power to hurt her again.

Tamera cleared her throat and began reading. "What are you doing here, Wyatt?" Her voice stumbled over the word and she looked up from the paper quickly.

"I'm here to apologize," a deep voice said from behind her.

Tamera whirled, her hand to her chest. Wyatt stood behind her in his football jersey, staring at her with those soulful brown eyes. Her eyes drank him in and she fought the urge to throw herself into his arms.

"Wyatt," she breathed.

A grin quirked up the corner of his mouth and he motioned to the script.

Right. The audition. Her eyes dropped back to the page, quickly finding her place. "Apologize for what?" she read.

He held a script in his own hands, but didn't look at it. "Apologize for letting you go. For not chasing after you and convincing you of the truth. I should've followed you to the airport and flown with you to San Antonio, if that's what it took."

Tamera blinked, trying to make out the words before her. "That would've been a little stalkerish."

His eyes danced with humor. "Okay, yeah. But I still should've tried harder to convince you of the truth."

Her eyes scanned the page and she read, her voice cracking. "I don't know what to believe anymore. Every guy I've ever opened my heart to has hurt me."

Wyatt took a step forward. Every hair on Tamera's body stood at attention and it was suddenly very hard to breathe.

"I know," he said, his voice a gentle caress. "And I understand why you ran. But I want to spend every day of the rest of my life proving that I'm a man worthy of your affections. Because I love you, Tamera."

The words were blurring before her, but she made out her one-sentence reply. "What do you love about me?"

Her reached out and tenderly tucked a strand of hair behind one ear. "I love the way your eyes light up when you talk about an audition you're excited for. I love debating films with you. I love the way the wind plays with your hair when you're driving your convertible. I love your laugh. I love how funny you are. I love a million tiny things that add up to a remarkable person who holds the key to my heart."

Tamera glanced down at the script and realized there was nothing more written on it. She dropped the stapled pages and they floated to the field.

"There's not an audition, is there?" she asked, making her voice teasing.

Wyatt chuckled and shook his head. "I wasn't sure how else to get you to listen to me."

"Well, at least I know you aren't acting. Because I've seen you try and you really do stink at it."

Another low rumble filled his chest. Tamera felt herself moving inexplicably closer. She rested her hands on his taut muscles and felt him tense beneath her palms.

"I'm sorry," she whispered, looking up at him. "I was so scared, and when I thought—"

He pressed a finger to her lips, cutting her off. "I'm the one who needs to apologize."

"You didn't do anything wrong."

"Not with Becky or with Drew," he conceded, inclining his head to the side. "But if I gave you any reason to doubt me, then I messed up.

Because I love you, Tamera. I've fallen completely, hopelessly in love with you. And I never want you to doubt that again."

Tamera closed her eyes as a sob of pure happiness tore through her. "I love you, too. I never doubted you, Wyatt—I doubted myself. Tonight I was going to fall on my knees and beg you to give me another chance, if that's what it took."

His fingers caressed her cheek, trailing fire with his touch. "I never would've made you grovel."

"I'm done second guessing myself," she whispered, staring up into his eyes. "I'm all in."

His arms wrapped around her waist and lifted her into the air. Tamera placed her hands on either side of Wyatt's face, feeling the slight scruff beneath them.

"I'm never letting you go again," Wyatt whispered.

"Me, either," Tamera said.

"I'm holding you to that," he said.

"Good." And then she pressed her lips to his, and neither of them said anything else for a very long time.

Epilogue

FOUR MONTHS LATER

"So then the cat went totally crazy," Tamera said. She sat in her favorite lounge chair at the back of Wyatt's home theater, looking way too adorable in her fitted jeans and fitted T-shirt.

Wyatt nodded, trying to focus on her story as his hands shook. "Didn't the animal trainer do anything?"

"No. I think she was in total shock or something. Anyway, the cat managed to step through the ranch dip on the food table and track it halfway across the studio before we caught him. The director was so upset he sent everyone home early so they could clean up the mess. It was insane."

Wyatt glanced into the tub of popcorn, making sure the ring box he'd hidden was completely covered by the freshly popped kernels and M&M's. He'd bought the ring nearly two months ago and had been working up the courage to spring the question on her ever since.

The guys on the team had been shocked at how quickly Wyatt and Tamera's relationship had moved. But to Wyatt, it felt like Tamera had always been a part of his life.

Wyatt carefully picked up the bucket and walked over to his favorite recliner, right beside Tamera's. In the four months since he'd moved in, they'd made frequent use of the room. After a spirited debate that ended in a very pleasant kissing session, they'd decided to start with the classic silent movies from the thirties and moved forward in time to where they currently were, the nineties. The age of romantic comedies, as Tamera liked to call it.

"I'm glad you're liking your new job so much," Wyatt said. The film was an independent project with a first-time director, but Tamera had been cast in the lead role. Wyatt had no doubt she'd slay it.

"So much better than selling houses." Tamera glanced around the theater room and grinned. "No offense. Anyway, how was your day?"

"Practice was great," Wyatt said. He handed her the tub of popcorn, struggling to keep the motion casual. His heart was going to beat out of his chest if he wasn't careful.

"So you really think you might make it to the finals this season, huh?"

"I think we have a good shot." The team had made remarkable progress over the summer, and their first game was next week.

"That's great, Wyatt. I'm so happy for you." She picked up an M&M from the popcorn and grinned. "Ooo, you put M&M's in it. Excellent."

"I know you like it that way," Wyatt said, struggling to keep his voice steady. Her hand dug into the popcorn and he held his breath. But she didn't find the ring box.

"I like M&M's in popcorn, but you don't." She leaned over and gave him a kiss on his cheek, sending his heart racing. "Thanks, babe. Did you hear back on the script you submitted yet?"

"Nothing yet," Wyatt said. He'd finally sent one to a director he was distantly acquainted with in Hollywood at Tamera's suggestion. Wyatt wasn't holding his breath—he knew the likelihood of selling the first script he ever pitched was minuscule. But he also knew that the thought of retiring from football no longer made him break out in a cold sweat. He'd enjoy his football career, however long it lasted. And when the time to retire finally came, he'd pursue screenwriting full-time.

"He's insane if he doesn't option it," Tamera said.

Wyatt kissed her on the head, feeling so much love for the woman sitting beside him that his heart felt like it might burst with happiness.

He glanced again at the popcorn tub and reached for the remote. "Should we start the movie?"

"Sure. What are we watching this time?"

"*Runaway Bride*," Wyatt said. Natalie had finally convinced him it was the perfect film for tonight.

"Awesome." Tamera snuggled into him as the opening credits started.

Wyatt tried his best to pay attention to the movie, but he kept eying the popcorn, monitoring how low the tub was getting. Maybe he should've placed it closer to the top, because this wait was going to kill him if the nerves didn't do it first.

Tamera was completely engrossed in the movie. She uncovered the ring box, and for a moment Wyatt's heart stopped beating as he waited for her to discover it. But her eyes never strayed from the screen and she grabbed a handful of popcorn, missing the ring box by centimeters.

As Ike made his romantic proposal to Maggie, Wyatt watched Tamera's eyes grow luminescent with tears. She reached into the popcorn and her hand finally—finally!—hit the ring box.

"What on earth?" She glanced down, her attention pulled away from the movie for the first time since it started, and held up the ring box.

This was it. Wyatt paused the movie and took the box gently from her hand, dropping to one knee.

"Tamera Hadley," he said quietly, flipping the box open. His hands shook, but he kept his voice steady.

"Oh my gosh," Tamera whispered, staring at him with wide eyes.

"I didn't write a script for this one," he said.

She laughed, and the sound was nearly as unsteady as his hands. His heart squeeze, like it had been wrapped in a warm hug.

"But I don't need a script to tell me I love you with my entire soul," Wyatt said. A dozen different sentences swirled through his mind, but none of them seemed adequate for this moment. He gulped, losing himself in her hazel eyes. Finally, he settled on the truth in it's simplest form. "I can't imagine spending the rest of my life with anyone else. Will you marry me?"

"Yes!" Tamera shrieked. "I was beginning to think you'd never ask. Yes, you crazy man."

Wyatt pulled the ring from the box and slipped it onto her finger, then pulled her close and kissed her soundly. Later, he'd tell her about how long ago he'd bought the ring. How he'd taken to carrying it around in his pocket, hoping for the perfect moment to ask her to be his. But right now, he wanted to savor this moment.

Tamera Hadley was going to be his wife. He brought her hand to his lips, the sight of his diamond ring on her left hand filling him with immense pride and happiness.

Tamera laughed, wrapping her arms around Wyatt's neck and pulling him close.

"I love you," she whispered.

He groaned, pulling her more tightly against him. "I love you too," he said.

And then he kissed her.

About the Author

LINDZEE ARMSTRONG is the *USA Today* bestselling and award-winning author of more than twenty-five romance novels. Like any true romantic, Lindzee loves chick flicks, ice cream, and chocolate. She believes in sigh-worthy kisses and happily ever afters, and loves expressing that through her writing. She and her Prince Charming are raising twin boys in the Rocky Mountains.

To find out about future releases, you can join Lindzee's newsletter. You can also find her on her website, www.LindzeeArmstrongBooks.com, and on most social media platforms.

If you enjoyed this book, it would be awesome if you'd leave a review wherever you read. It really helps other readers discover books they might enjoy (and totally makes the author's day, too). Thank you!

www.ingramcontent.com/pod-product-compliance
Lightning Source LLC
Chambersburg PA
CBHW032004240626
47153CB00003B/1111